Praise for *Trouble Is What I Do*

'This gifted raconteur of the African American experience has produced an absorbing noir beauty of a tale'

Richard Lipez, *Washington Post*

'A slim volume with the feel of a fable and the concision of a blues scale. Minor characters have marvelous names – Archibald Lawless, Dido Kazz, Mozelle Tot – and move with ageless grace. "I felt a kinship to all of them," Leonid thinks. So do we'

Wall Street Journal

'The charms of this short novel lie in Mosley's memorable characters, his portrayal of the world McGill inhabits and the author's uniquely lyrical writing style'

Associated Press

'A tight and quietly subversive tale about family, class, privilege, and race (plus honor, of all things) that packs a hard tight punch. You won't see it coming, but you'll know when it lands'

Mystery Scene Magazine

'[Mosley] wanders through a few underworlds of the New York City crime category, always a treat for readers, and one that packs a moral punch. Mosley is, quite simply, an icon of detective fiction, and with each new novel in the McGill series he's making New York noir his own just as he did with Los Angeles'   *LitHub*

'Spieled in a powerful, streamlined voice, this wrenching American noir will stick with readers long after the final page'   *Booklist*

'Watching McGill coolly deploy the physical and intellectual skills he'd acquired in his previous life as an underworld "fixer" provides the principal pleasure of this installment ---- with Mosley's own way of maki--   ---- blues ballad . . . M   ow a master's at w   *irkus*

TROUBLE IS
WHAT I DO

WALTER MOSLEY

WEIDENFELD & NICOLSON

First published in the United States in 2020 by Mulholland Books,
an imprint of Little, Brown and Company,
a division of Hachette Book Group, Inc.

First published in Great Britain in 2020 by Weidenfeld & Nicolson
This paperback edition published in 2020 by Weidenfeld & Nicolson
an imprint of the Orion Publishing Group Ltd
Carmelite House, 50 Victoria Embankment,
London EC4Y 0DZ

An Hachette UK Company

1 3 5 7 9 10 8 6 4 2

A CIP catalogue record for this book is available
from the British Library

Printed and bound in Great Britain by Clays Ltd, Elcograf S.p.A.

ISBN (Mass Market Paperback) 978 1 4746 1654 6
ISBN (eBook) 978 1 4746 1655 3

www.orionbooks.co.uk
www.weidenfeldandnicolson.co.uk

This book is dedicated to the unseen people
and unknown places of
New York City

TROUBLE IS WHAT I DO

"MR. MCGILL?" MARDI BITTERMAN said over the intercom that connects her desk at the front of our office complex to mine at the far end.

I lease a very large office space, but as of yet only Mardi and sometimes my son Twill work there with me. She's the detective agency's secretary-receptionist and also the human barometer that helps maintain my moral bearings in a world where sin is reflex and kindness a quick death. Mardi has firsthand experience with the evil that men visit upon children and absolutely no fear of losing her own life or witnessing the death of someone who deserves it. In my opinion she's a saint; in hers, I and my son are saviors.

Twill is another thing altogether. Though he also understands the rising tide of depravity and violence, my son is like a futuristic fish in those waters, a sleek metallic shark evolved beyond other species. He is the youngest of the three children who call me father. My wife claims that he's mine, but I know that only the eldest boy, Dimitri, is of my blood. Not that I mind. I love them all.

"Yes, Mardi?" I said into the speaker box.

"There are people here to see you," she said softly. "Shall I bring them back?"

"Sure."

We had a simplistic code system. The first sentence was plain fact, the second phrase for me to decipher. For instance: If she asked if these *people* had an appointment, I'd know that it was an official visitation, most likely the police. If she asked, "Should I make an appointment?" I'd know that they might be dangerous and I should look through the video monitor that watched over her desk. From there, I could assess any threat.

But the offer to walk them back meant that these potential clients were all right and I should treat them as such.

I took the snub-nosed .38 from my pencil drawer and pocketed it. Mardi's intuition of human nature and potential was better than mine—but she wasn't infallible.

Opening the door to my office, I looked down the triple-wide hallway that was flanked by six desks on either side. One day I'd run a real detective agency—I had the seats. But that morning, there was only Twill standing midway down the hall at his laptop podium. He wore dark navy pants and a sky-blue collarless jacket. His shirt was pink.

Long and handsome, slender and strong, my black-skinned eighteen-year-old son was studying the computer screen, looking for blowback on one of his misadventures, material for his next scam, or maybe even one of the cases I'd asked him to peruse.

Twill noticed me standing sentry and turned just in time to see pale-skinned and slight Mardi coming through the inner door that connected to her reception-ist's area. Immediately in her wake came a tall young man carrying a battered guitar case. He was a few years older than Twill. Behind the youth, a senior citizen trundled lightly. The young man had chocolate-brown skin. His el-der was what they called *redbone* back in the day. The expression had lately come back into usage. It described a light-skinned Negro. They both wore new blue jeans, checkered blue work shirts, and hard leather shoes that had counted more miles than a Fitbit could imagine.

The older gentleman carried a rather incongruous aluminum briefcase; this, I decided, contained the reason for their impromptu visit. Maybe they were sharecroppers on holiday, decked out in their party clothes and laden with the weight of some legal entanglement that required a big-city specialist who was brown of skin and ready to rumble.

As the trio passed, Twill moved out into the aisle, no doubt to make sure that no trouble accompanied the men. Mardi placed a hand on my son-protector's arm, whispered a word or two, and he stood back.

The older man, a few inches taller than my five foot five and five-eighths inches, had taken the lead. He stopped in front of me. I'd almost hit sixty on my last birthday. My father had twenty years on that. The man facing me was hale and healthy, but he could have been my father's father — if he started young.

I held out a hand and said, "Leonid McGill."

He reached out and drawled, "I were born Philip Worry, but they been callin' me Catfish since 1941. This here is my great-great-grandson Lamont Richards."

"Pleased to meet you," the younger obliged.

The descendant and I shook hands. He was about six foot and my walking-around weight, which is 182 pounds. I'm a light heavyweight in pounds and muscle, intentions and training.

"Pleased to meet you, Lamont, Catfish. Why don't you two come on in and take a seat." Mardi was turning to go back to her post when I added, "You too, Mardi. I'd like you to take notes."

The child of misery grinned, following the men into the office.

I HAD TO MOVE boxes of files off a couple of chairs to get everybody seated. I like writing down how I solve, resolve, or fail at the jobs I've taken on. And writing by hand I seem to remember better than when entering data on a computer screen.

As the men and Mardi claimed blue visitors' chairs, I lowered into my swivel seat. Through the window behind me, there on the seventy-second floor of the Tesla Building, you could see all the way to Wall Street and the fading memory of the Twin Towers.

"You got a nice office here, Mr. McGill," Catfish complimented. His left eye was dead and fogged over. Oddly, this infirmity gave off an air of inner ecstasy. There was a sleek scar under the blind eye; maybe that wound had something to do with its demise.

"You got a good grip too," he added. "You ever work on a farm?"

"My father's people were sharecroppers. Me—I get it from the boxing gym."

"You box?" the great-great-grandson asked.

"Not professionally. Not anymore. But I can throw haymakers when I have to. You got a strong hand too, Lamont."

"I string tennis rackets for white people at the country club an' play guitar behind C-Paw when I can."

Mardi had taken up the notebook and pencil kept next to the in-box. She jotted our first words down.

"What can I do for you men?" I asked.

"I hear you the kind'a brothah-man been on both sides'a the line," Catfish offered.

"Who told you that?"

"Pinky Eckles."

A chill ran from the back of my neck down through my left foot.

"Is this Pinky somehow related to a man named Ernie Eckles?"

"She birthed him."

MY MIND RANGED BACK over a decade earlier. Ernie Eckles was a unique individual in my experience, and I have met all kinds of men and women, from tragic billionaires to serial killers swathed in the light of innocence.

Ernie was known in certain circles as the Mississippi Assassin—and that was not the name of a professional wrestler. He was of average height and normal build, with medium-brown skin. He was as country as a bale of cotton on an unwilling child's back. His price when I knew him was seven thousand seven hundred and forty-eight dollars to kill anyone, anywhere in North America. This price covered all of Ernie's expenses, from the bus ticket down to the cost of three bullets.

Ernie could hide naked in a snowstorm or talk a blushing bride out of her virginity on her wedding day—at least that's how the stories have it. He never missed, never failed—that much was fact. If he had your name scribbled on the back of his bus ticket, you were as good as dead.

Along the way, the Mississippi Assassin had been hired to kill a young Brooklynite named Patrice Sandoval. Sandoval had been fingered as the mastermind of the hijacking of six tons of marijuana that had been grown, processed, and packaged by Merle Underman, a son of Texas so far back that his ancestors lived there when that state was a sovereign nation.

Eckles had been engaged on a Monday evening, so, after consulting a Greyhound bus schedule, I put him at Port Authority by Wednesday—late afternoon. He had twenty-four hours to shoot Mr. Sandoval three times and get back on a bus home. That's how it would have happened, except for the fact that the victim of the heist,

Mr. Underman, was a boastful sort. He bragged to his lieutenant, Rexford Brothers, that Sandoval had an unscheduled meeting with the reaper called Eckles. Even that should have been fine, but Merle didn't know that Brothers, working through a modern-day highwayman named Shorty Reeves, was the one behind the hijacking. Shorty took the truck down with a crew of two. When Shorty was told by Rexford that the blame would fall on Sandoval, the self-styled desperado told his accomplices that they were safe and could start spending their ill-gotten gains.

One of the crew, Phil Thomas, had recently made the acquaintance of a civilian named Minda Myles. Minda was a very religious young woman who wanted to save her lover's soul. She implored him to warn Sandoval, saving the innocent man's life and Phil's afterlife.

Beatrice Fitz, Phil's mom, was a bookie I knew. Phil went to her, and she called me. I owed Beatrice a favor, and so, without proper study, I agreed to take the job.

I'd never heard of Eckles, but I had friends who had. Once I knew what I was up against, I regretted saying yes to Bea, but even back then, when I was still mostly a crook, I had pride in my work and was known as a man of my word.

Beatrice gave me a general lowdown on Sandoval. I made a few phone calls, then took the F train to Coney Island and dropped by a café frequented by a certain element of drug dealer.

THERE WAS A YOUNG man wearing a flower-patterned shirt and yellow sunglasses sitting at a round table toward the center of the dining room. I knew from Beatrice's description that this was Patrice Sandoval. He had fair skin and hair the color of finished maple wood. His eyes were a light color I couldn't immediately identify through the yellow lenses.

He sat there comfortably watching me approach. There were six or seven other men standing or sitting and a waitress who sat face-out from the counter, watching me. They were all white and very aware that I was not. This didn't bother me much. I'd sent a message through a friend of mine that I, Timothy Lothar, was interested in buying one hundred pounds of primo ganja. Patrice was a dope dealer. That's why he was so easy to finger for the Underman heist.

"Mr. Sandoval," I said upon reaching his table.

"Mr. Lothar?"

I nodded.

"Is that your real name?"

"It is today," I replied, pulling out a chair.

"I hear from Fred Fox that you want a serious taste."

"That's nothing compared to what you'll want after hearing me out, Patrice."

The handsome young drug dealer's face took on a serious cast. He must have made a gesture of some sort, because two guys at a table across from us looked up and seemed ready for action.

I'm a pretty good scrapper and I had gone armed to that meeting, but that's not why I wasn't nervous. The truth is, if a man in my line of work got nervous, he'd die of a heart attack before anyone got the chance to cave in his skull.

"I don't get what you mean," Patrice Sandoval said, his affable smile now packed away.

"Somebody recently whispered a name in my ear," I said. "That name is Ernie Eckles."

"That s'posed to mean something to me?" Patrice's bland expression would have represented the soul of innocence if he were not a drug dealer in a den of thieves.

"He works out of Mississippi," I said. "Right now he's on a job for a guy named Underman. He's from Dallas–Fort Worth."

Patrice sat back in his chair.

The two thugs stood up. This made me smile. I was a younger man then, always ready for a good tussle. They rolled up on us, looking tough. One was fat and half a foot taller than I. The other was thin and six inches taller than his fat friend.

"What's your name?" the shorter man asked me.

"Hey, True," Patrice said, "we know a guy named Underman from Texas?"

"Why?" the fat man named for veracity asked.

"How about a guy named Ernie Eckles?"

True had a ruddy complexion, but his face blanched a bit when he heard that name spoken aloud.

"You come on with me, Patty," he said. And to me: "You wait here."

I had nowhere to be. The tall, skinny man and a few of his friends came to stand around and block my exit—if I suddenly lost nerve and ran.

"Excuse me, miss," I called to the waitress.

"Yeah?" She was entering her forties and lovely at that age. Brown hair dyed blond and eyes the color of blue steel. I believed that she was probably the kind of woman to stand by you when the chips were down.

Funny the things one pays attention to when death is hovering nearby.

"Can I get a cup of coffee?" I asked her.

"Oh. Sure. Milk and sugar?"

"Black," I said, and she gave me a half smile that went deeper than a laugh.

"You better have some sugar," a short thug remarked. He had skin the color of ivory from a fresh poacher's kill and wore a square-cut blue shirt with lacquer-brown pants.

"Why's that?" I asked, as close to ingenuous as I could manage.

The waitress had moved behind the counter to fill my order.

"Because you should have something sweet for your last meal," the thug replied.

"I kill you first," I stated.

He moved his shoulder in such a way that alarmed the tall, skinny guy enough that he put a hand on the short man's shoulder.

The waitress walked up then with a big white mug filled with steaming black coffee.

"What's your name?" I asked her.

Those blue eyes shone like headlights upon the perpetual darkness of her life.

"You don't give a shit, do you, mister?"

"I tried to but nobody seems to want it."

She laughed and said, "Sheila. Sheila Normandy."

"Leonid McGill. I'm in the book."

"Me too."

At that moment the fat man called True returned. Behind him, about ten feet away at the counter, stood Patrice.

"Who the fuck are you, brother?" True asked. He was standing over me.

"Have a seat," I offered.

He gave me a hard stare but then relented. He took the chair that Patrice had abandoned. Putting both elbows on the table, True laced his fat fingers under tented thumbs.

"Okay," he said. "Now what's this shit about Ernie Eckles?"

"Somebody decided that your boy Patrice looked good for the theft of six tons of product from Underman. This somebody told Underman that Patrice was the mastermind. Underman told Eckles."

True was not happy. His mouth twisted from a foul taste.

"When?" he asked.

"When did he tell Ernie? Monday afternoon, as close as I can figure."

"He'll be on him tonight."

"Quite likely."

"What's that got to do with you?" True asked.

"I've been retained by an anonymous client to protect Patrice if I can."

"Paid by who?"

"I said retained, not paid. And anonymous means I don't say."

True would have liked to stomp me with the hardest shoes in his closet. He'd've been happy to see me in the ground. That's the kind of response imminent death has on men who live by intimidation.

We studied each other's eyes until the fat man accepted the fact that he was in over his depth.

"You know Eckles?"

"I know what they say he can do."

"And you still took the job?"

"You should hear what they say about me."

True was wearing a one-button gray suit that had been tailored for his bulk twenty pounds ago. He leaned back, putting serious strain on that solitary button. His eyes focused on me with a look that was both diabolical and afraid—a bad combination.

"Patty," he called, his eyes still on me.

The pretty boy came to our table and sat.

"You say you don't know nuthin' 'bout Underman?" True asked his minion.

"No," Patrice answered. "I never even heard the name before today."

The fat man glanced at Patrice, then glared at me.

"Anyone else on Eckles's list?"

"Patrice is the only name I'm concerned with." It wasn't a great answer, but it was the best I had.

"And how do you plan to protect him?"

"Protect me from what?" Patrice wanted to know.

"I think it would be better to keep my plans on the need-to-know," I said. "That way if something goes wrong, I won't have to come looking for you."

True paused again, trying to figure out if I had somehow insulted him. Then he said, "Patty."

"Yeah, True?"

"I think you should go with this guy."

"Go with him? I don't even know him."

True leveled his dark eyes at Patrice's pale orbs.

"His name is Leonid McGill and he's a fixer. Works for people like my boss's boss. And if Eckles is really after you, he's the only long shot you got."

That was quite a while ago. Back then, I relied on my reputation. I was surprised, however, that my name had made it all the way out to Coney Island.

The affable young man and I went to the counter, where I handed Sheila Normandy a ten-dollar bill. She smiled and handed it back along with a slip of paper that bore a phone number. That phone number got me a night of bliss, a broken wrist, and, in the end, it cost a man his life. But that's another story.

I GOT PATRICE SANDOVAL to the Alonzo at about 4:00. It was a cheap dive that had rooms by the day or the hour. I went in first and was given the key to 2D. I found the room, put my empty suitcase down, and then went to the Glacier Bar across the street. Maybe twenty minutes later, as instructed, Patrice came into the joint and joined me at a table near the jukebox.

He put a key down and said, "Four-A. I left the bag you gave me up there."

I slid my door key across to him.

"Call your mother and True," I said. "Tell them both that you're staying at the Alonzo. Tell 'em both that it's no secret you're there. Make sure they know you're in room 4A."

"But I thought I was gonna take your room."

"You are."

I don't think he understood what I was planning, but he promised to make the calls and give the right room number—that was all I needed.

We had drinks, over which I explained to him my plan. He was going to go downstairs and tell the man at the front desk that he would be out but to tell his friends that he'd be back by midnight.

"I don't get it," he said.

"What's to get?"

"All somebody has to do is tell somebody my name, and then they send someone to kill me?"

"If you have to ask that question, you should probably consider a new line of work."

Soon after that, we retired to our switched rooms.

If Eckles was as good as they said, he'd show up before long.

I WAS SITTING IN the dark at a few minutes past nine when there came the slightest rustle and click at the door. I really shouldn't have been in the room at all. It would have been better to wait in 4C, across the hall, keeping vigil until my quarry arrived. But I was young, not yet fifty, and overconfident. Still, I was smart enough to wait in the dark and to the side. So when the door came open and the shadow figure passed through, I lunged forward, throwing a beautifully timed left hook. But Mr. Eckles had preternatural reflexes. As fast as I was, he pulled away so that my fist barely glanced his shoulder. He grunted and allowed his weight to bear him away from me. I stayed on him, though, unloading a right, a left, and another right in his direction. And damn if he didn't slip every blow. When he fired back, I felt it in my jaw, shoulder, and gut. If I wasn't in shape from regular workouts at Gordo's boxing gym, that would have been the end for me. As it was, I had to push through the pain and disorientation. He was too good for me to rely on my pugilism skills, so I heaved my 182 pounds in the middleweight's direction. He fell beneath the weight, and I rained down blows at his head. Of the first five punches, only two connected, but the last one stunned him. I hit him five more times, enough to kill a regular guy, and even then I was prepared for him to come back at me.

When I was sure that he was out, I searched his clothes for a gun, found it, then went to close the door and turn the switch. . . . The overhead light revealed the Mississippi Assassin risen to one knee and pulling a hunting knife from a sheath on his leg. I rushed over and hit him with his own gun butt—repeatedly.

AN HOUR OR SO later, Ernie Eckles opened his eyes. He was chained by handcuffs and ankle bracelets to the strongest chair in the room. The chair was itself chained to the cast-iron radiator. There was half a pillowcase stuffed in his mouth with electrician's tape holding the gag in place.

I say that he opened his eyes an hour later because I had the feeling he'd regained consciousness sometime before that.

"Mr. Eckles?"

Those dark eyes scanned the room, photographed my face, and then they hardened.

"I want to take the gag out and I don't want to slap you upside the head with this gun again," I said, showing him the pistol.

He considered the offer, waited a moment, and then nodded.

I pulled off the tape as gently as I could.

"You can work the gag out with your tongue. I wouldn't wanna get bit or some shit like that."

It was hard to make out, but I think the crack about him biting me elicited a smile. He spat out the rag, then took in a deep breath through his mouth. The left side of Ernie's jaw was slightly swollen.

His eyes went out of focus, communicating that he would wait for me to start. Instead I went to the house phone near the bed and dialed a 9 and then a phone number.

"Hello?" a scared voice asked.

"Come on up," I said.

No more than ten minutes later, there came a knock. Patrice Sandoval wore black cotton trousers, a coral shirt, and a forest-green sports jacket. I remember thinking that he'd make a good-looking corpse.

The young man was visibly shaken when he saw Ernie staring at him.

"He's still alive?"

"I was asked to save your life—not take his," I told him. Then I turned to my prisoner. "Mr. Eckles, I'd like to introduce you to your target—Patrice Sandoval."

The way Ernie glared at him reminded me that a caged tiger was still a tiger.

"What you want?" Ernie's voice was a surprisingly pleasant tenor. I would have bet that he exercised it in a Sunday choir down home.

"You have to understand, Mr. Eckles," I explained. "I don't usually mess with a man's destination. As a matter of fact I never do, unless one of the tires is soft and he's on a treacherous road."

"If that there is Sandoval, and I know it is, then all my tires is hard and aligned."

"You would think so," I replied, "but this is not the man that stole Mr. Underman's weed."

"I don't care about 'he said, she said,'" Eckles preached. "I got a job to do."

"And that's where I believe there might be room for negotiation."

"Are you gonna kill him or what?" Patrice wanted to know.

"What's your name?" Eckles asked me.

"It is an exhibition of deepest respect that I do not answer that question, Mr. Eckles."

He smirked and asked, "What's the negotiation?"

"Rexford Brothers by way of Shorty Reeves."

"Shorty?" Patrice piped. "What's Shorty got to do with this?"

Keeping my eye on Eckles, I said, "Brothers is Underman's number two. He decided to rip off his boss by telling the said Shorty Reeves about a six-ton delivery coming up through North Carolina. Shorty took down the truck, gave Brothers his cut and the name of Patrice here. I'm quite sure that Mr. Underman would like his seven thousand seven hundred forty-eight dollars doing the right work."

The Mississippi Assassin remained silent, but I could see that my words had made an impression on him. I knew too much about the heist and the hit.

For a minute or two more, Ernie glared and Patrice fidgeted. Then I took a small amber bottle and another piece of pillowcase from a pocket.

While pouring the right amount of ether on the cloth, I said, "I'm putting you to sleep now, Ernie. Once again, this is a show of respect. When you wake up, I hope you think on what I said."

I draped the cloth over his nose and mouth, careful to hold the lower part below his chin—so that he didn't turn tiger and bite off a finger. After the killer had passed out, I took off the shackles and the unconscious body slumped to the floor.

"We should kill him," Patrice said.

I slapped the handsome young man hard enough that he stumbled backward, all the way to the far wall.

Then I said, "Let's go."

I DROVE PATRICE TO his mother's house in Queens, on the way explaining that he should disappear, preferably somewhere out of state, until such a time that I made sure Underman was off his ass.

"How will I know that?"

"I'll get word to True."

THE FALLOUT WAS PRETTY quick. Four days after I left Patrice with his mom, I read in the online version of the *Fort Worth Star-Telegram* that Rexford Brothers was found dead in his own mother's home. He had been shot three times.

The *New York Post* announced Shorty Reeves's

demise. Phil Thomas and Minda Myles had eloped and were on their honeymoon in Jamaica. I told Bea that it might be good for them to extend their vacation for a while.

THREE WEEKS LATER, I was going to my cubbyhole of an office, which was, at the time, on the ninth floor of the Joseph T. Banner Building on West Thirty-First Street. It was thirteen past seven in the evening when I used the four keys on six locks, in the proper order, and walked in.

By then, it was already too late.

I closed the door and said aloud, "You see why I didn't want to tell you my name?"

I couldn't see him, but he was there.

"Just keep your hands away from your sides," the Mississippi Assassin warned.

It took a while, but finally I was seated behind my desk. Ernie reclined in my speckled green-and-white client's chair, pistol in hand. He had on a well-worn army jacket, brown pants and shoes.

"You the first one ever caught me off guard," he said. "An' that's sayin' sumpin'. 'Specially cause'a where I was an' what I was doin'. You taught me a real lesson there, Leonid McGill."

I wondered what kind of education he had in store for me.

"You a drinkin' man?" Ernie asked.

"I like the good stuff. All except scotch. I can't stand scotch."

With his free hand, he brought a clear glass jar from a deep pocket. The jar was filled with amber liquid and secured with a screw-on lid.

He said, "This here is one-hundred-forty-seven-year-old corn liquor aged in a charred-oak cask. You know what that means?"

The moonshine had an inner light that danced like laughter.

"Bourbon," I said.

"You got glasses?"

"You must know. I don't think you'd have me sitting here if you hadn't checked out the drawers."

I pulled out two bowled glasses.

He pushed the jar toward me and said, "Pour us two stiff ones."

I entertained the idea of splashing the whiskey in his eyes or ducking down and flipping my pine desk at him. But if Eckles was dangerous in the dark with his back turned, then he'd be death sitting before me, straight on, in the light, and with a gun in his hand.

So I poured our drinks, then took a sip. It was, hands down, the best liquor I had ever tasted. My expression said this, and Ernie Eckles cracked a smile.

"My great-great-grandfather bunged it in twenty-three barrels. There's still seven left. I take a jar every Christmas and sip at it all year."

I took another taste. It was so smooth that I imagined a green snake slithering across an emerald lawn.

"Underman didn't like what I had to say, but he listened," Ernie recounted. "You owe me for that. But the job is over. Kid is safe."

"It's over?"

"That's what I said, ain't it?"

"No more bodies?"

He studied my question and then nodded like he did the evening I offered him his life. Then he finished his drink, rose from the chair, and secreted the gun somewhere under his jacket.

Seeing him walk out the door was the deepest relief I have ever experienced.

ELEVEN YEARS LATER, I was sitting with Catfish Worry and Lamont Richards, still breathing and still afraid of just the name Eckles.

"So what is it you want from me, Mr. Worry?"

The old man grinned. He had a full complement of big yellow choppers. Nodding as if to the music of his own guitar, he laid the briefcase flat on the desk, popped the latches, flipped it open, and turned the contents to me.

The body of the attaché held a mason jar nestled in bunched-up burlap. The hanging file above carried a large manila folder.

"Is that Eckles's bourbon?" I asked.

"One hunnert an' fifty-eight year old. It's yours if you could get this envelope into the right hands."

When I reached for the folder, Catfish stiffened and held up a hand.

"Hold up, brother," he said. "Ain't nobody seen what's in here for sixty-six years."

"You've seen it."

"I cain't read. Never could."

"But you held on to it for all this time?"

"Made a promise to a lady."

Catfish Worry was a good-looking man even at his great age. There was character in his deeply lined face and something profound emanating from his one good eye. I imagined that he'd known many dozens of women but not so many that he'd forget a promise. This made me think of my own father; of how he had failed me and my brother, our mother, and even his own cause.

"What promise?"

"That if she died and when the time came, if it came, that there was a girl-child born outta her heirs, that I would give that child the letter in here when she'd need it."

"I don't see where I fit into that," I said. "I mean, if all you need to do is hand a folder to someone, then why don't you just ring their doorbell?"

"The young lady we talkin' 'bout is Justine Penelope Sternman." Catfish's stare was almost as serious as the name he'd uttered.

Justine Penelope Sternman was daughter to Charles Augustus Sternman. The family business was a private bank that held assets greater than most large banks in America. Charles had been an adviser to three presidents, and he was granted honorary citizenship in South Africa when apartheid was all the rage. In an interview, he'd called Nigeria a shithole and its president a *nigger in a hat*. When there were protests, he simply stated, "In America we believe in free speech."

The Sternmans' long-ago ancestress Georgina Soule started a private club called the Sisterhood of the *Mayflower*: an exclusive group of women descended from that select crowd of Puritan Pilgrims. Justine was the next in line for the leadership of that organization. She was also slated to wed Andrew Printer, a South Carolinian whom Charles intended to take over the Sternman empire when he was through with it.

"I see," I said. "That's some name. It might make sense, you coming to me."

"Will you do it?" the man named for a freshwater bottom-feeder asked.

"I have to know what's in any letter I deliver. I mean, you seem like a good guy and all, but this might be blackmail, or worse."

Catfish squinted, understanding my words.

"May I?" I asked, gesturing at the folder in his briefcase.

Hesitating, he said, "I know. You don't wanna buy a pig in a poke. Okay. Lamont and me'll wait outside while you read what it has to say."

He stood up, and Lamont followed suit. Mardi waited a moment, and then she rose too.

"I'll go with them," she said, "in case they need something."

Before she pulled the door closed, I was taking a glass from my bottom drawer. It was one of the same glasses I'd used with the Mississippi Assassin years before.

I knew from the aroma that it was the same batch. Ernie was reaching out to tell me that Catfish was the debt I owed.

To my Granddaughter,

My name is Lucinda Pitts-Sternman, descended from the Puritans that came over on the Mayflower, *daughter of Norferd Sternman and Edwina Marlene Pitts. I was born of what my father's line calls the best blood. We were the kernel of everything this nation has become— both right and wrong. Victims of religious oppression, my ancestors laid the foundation for what they called the greatest democracy ever to exist. I believed them until the day I met Philip Worry, called Catfish by his friends. Mr. Worry was a traveling musician down on his luck along the Grand Concourse near my parents' home in the Bronx. He'd known my father's butler, Archer Mandell, from a club in Manhattan. Archer convinced my father to hire Mr. Worry as our summer gardener. Archer and Mr. Worry, Catfish, are both Negroes.*

One night I came across Catfish playing guitar in the garden house where he lived. He was kind enough to teach me how to play a few chords on his guitar. It was a music I'd never heard before. Every after-noon when I was at home, and my parents were not, Catfish taught me how to play that most exhilarating music. We became quite intimate. And then one day my father found us. Luckily we were just playing our guitars. *Catfish was showing me the fingering of a complex chord progression.*

Father took up one of his walking canes and beat my friend until I thought he was dead. When I tried to intervene, my father struck me with the back of his hand, knocking me to the floor. After that, he had Archer throw Catfish in the alley that ran behind our house.

That night I locked and barricaded the door to my bedroom and cried. I wept and threw tantrums, sulked, and slowly came to the decision to take my own life. I have no doubt that I would have committed this mortal sin if there hadn't come a knocking on the door leading to the private patio that overlooks the summer garden. Catfish had somehow dragged himself from the alley and climbed up the trellis. He was bruised, battered, and bleeding. His left eye was severely damaged. It never healed. When I saw him, I knew that God was telling me not to commit a crime but to rectify one. While I washed his wounds and gave him what succor I could, my father came to the door and pounded on it, probably with the same cane that he almost killed my teacher, my lover, with. I yelled that I would not let him in and furthermore I would be leaving for London to stay with my aunt, Alice Heath. The words came from my mouth like Athena from Zeus's brow—wisdom born of pain.

Catfish had fever for five days. I only accepted food from our young maid, Minerette, Archer's daughter. Through her I got bandages and other medical supplies and solidified plans to leave the country. Using monies left in trust for me by my suffragette grandmother, I paid for our passage and left the house through the same window Catfish used to come to me.

My love for Philip Worry only grew stronger over that period. He spoke no word against my father because he preferred to suffer that beating rather than to kill the father of the woman who carried his child.

He was married. He loved his wife, Ernestine, with a passion that only comes once in a lifetime. He wrote her saying that he'd fallen ill and that his employer brought him to England for medical treatment. He stayed for the birth so that he could take our child home to Mississippi. He knew how difficult it would be for a colored child to stay in my world.

When Charles Augustus was born, he had white skin. I was overjoyed, but Catfish told me that Negro children often get their color in the weeks after their birth. But our son had blue eyes like so many of my kin and his skin darkened but a little. I convinced Catfish that a child that looked like ours would fare better in my world. He didn't agree but told me that he would never take a child from its mother. I named our son Sternman after our family and looked forward to keeping something of the man I loved in his progeny.

And so, my female heir, I write this letter in case I don't make it to your birth. It is the women who carry the bloodline. It is the women who hold the family secrets. And so I say to you, Granddaughter, you are the descendant of the men and women who shed blood, sweat, and tears on this land, all of those people. As you know, I have written this note on the back sheet of Susana Allan's journal. This document is unknown to the general public and therefore proof of my claims. I give you the truth and only ask that you look into your heart and know who you are.

Lucinda Pitts-Sternman

I reread the letter six times. The paper's color, once cream, now tended toward brown, but still it was quite durable. I assumed it was made from rag and not wood, probably linen. It had been cut along the side, lending credibility to the claim that it came from some ancient journal. The language that the honored ancestor used was definitely English, but with the exception of a few words, it was not immediately clear what she'd been writing about. At some other time, I would have spent the day at the Forty-Second Street library explicating the content. But I had orders straight from Ernie Eckles, and so the luxury of intellectual curiosity would have to wait.

MY PHONE BROWSER TOLD me that Lucinda Pitts-Sternman died in a car accident on Long Island in 1969. Her blue-eyed son was raised by his grandfather, Norferd Joseph Sternman—the man who blinded Catfish's left eye.

The child grew into an industrialist who didn't seem to care much about his unknown origins. Charles and his wife, Elizabeth Falsworth, had a daughter named Justine. Elizabeth had died of a heart attack not long after her daughter's birth.

TWILL AND LAMONT WERE sitting at Twill's station in the hall of desks. Lamont was dark-skinned, but my son was nearly black—being the offspring of a Malian diplomat whom my blond-haired, blue-eyed wife had fancied. I knew from my own experience that Lucinda Sternman's claim of having a white son from an interracial coupling could well be true.

"Where's Mr. Worry?" I asked the young men.

"Up in front with Mardi," Twill said.

"Yeah, up front," Lamont added.

*   *   *

I FOUND MY MORAL anchor and Catfish sitting at the small round table Mardi bought at a street flea market. She said it was something to put water on if a client got thirsty while waiting for me. She'd made coffee and brought out chairs for them to sit on.

When I came through the door, Mardi stood and said, "Would you like coffee, Mr. McGill?"

She served me and then left us to discuss the case.

"You read it?" Catfish asked when we were alone.

"You knew Justine's grandmother as a young man?"

"Lamont nor nobody else don't know nuthin' 'bout it. I mean, he knows I got a letter from a rich white lady to give to her granddaughter, but that's all."

"Because of Ernestine?"

Catfish looked down and shook his head.

"I loved Ernestine somethin' fierce," he said. "And she did me. We stayed together till she died six years past. But still, I had never known a white woman like Lucinda. She could play blues and drank whiskey, laugh like a lark sangin' and she didn't care one whit about color. I knew better than to mess wit' her, but what we know an' what we do ain't always the same thing."

"How old are you, Mr. Worry?"

"Ninety-four last November."

"And when did you meet Lucinda?"

"Nineteen and forty-nine in the early summer."

"After all this time, why do you feel that you need to deliver this letter to your granddaughter?"

"I'm agin it," the old man said with emphasis.

"Then why do it? I mean, I didn't see anything in there that would benefit her, her father, her fiancé, or their children."

"I believe you, Mr. McGill. You right. But I promised Lu that if our son had a daughter, I'd deliver that there note before she had a child of her own."

"But you don't even know what she says."

"An' I don't wanna know. A woman got the right to pass on whatever wisdom she want to her girl-chirren. A man got the same right with his sons."

The coffee was good. It went well with the ancient bootleg liquor still flitting around my taste buds.

"But Mr. Worry—"

"Call me Catfish."

"Catfish. Why do you feel that you had to ask me to pass along this letter? Don't get me wrong, I'll do it, if only because I owe Ernie a debt, but, you know, a man doesn't want to walk into something that might not be what it seems."

Strains of guitar music came through the door to the office proper.

Catfish Worry looked me in the eye, and I was glad to have asked the question. I was reminded that you didn't need to know how to read to be smart enough to engage in subterfuge.

"I should'a done what Lu aksed me to do," the bluesman admitted. "Just followed Justine around until I could get her alone somewhere an' give her what her grandmother wrote. But on the way, I got the desire to see my son. I mean, you see, Mr. McGill, I been all 'round this world. I played blues on the beach of the Pacific Ocean and in a club in Berlin not a mile from where Adolf Hitler kilt his wife an' his dog.... Somewhere along the way, I realized that skin color or jest the idea of some kinda race is a sickness comin' from the guilt and the fear of white men an' women. They know they wrong, but they jest cain't change up."

"And that has to do with your son?" I asked.

"My son think he a white man. He went to Harvard for a education and flew to China on his own supersonic plane. They say he hate black peoples, but I know that that's because I left him an' his mama. I left him ignorant of who he is, an' now he hate hisself an' don't even know it."

"So you went to tell him." It wasn't a question.

"He my son, my flesh and blood."

A strong male voice accompanied the blues guitar that reverberated through the inner office door. The voice sang a few words and then cut off.

"What did he say?" I asked. "Your son?"

Catfish regarded me with sincere regret in his eye. He shook his head again, made as if he was going to stand up and walk out rather than to confess his stupidity.

"He threatened to have me killed." There was a note of incredulity in Worry's voice.

"Killed?" The concept was a surprise and it wasn't.

"I think he might'a done it right there, but we were in the public space down on the first floor of his buildin'. I came up to him and told him my name. Then I said, 'You might not believe this, but you and me share blood, we related.' He told me if I ever said that again that he'd have me killed. Then he told his two bodyguards to grab me, but Lamont come up behind an' laid them low."

"Had you ever been in touch with him before?" I asked.

"No. That was the only time."

"Did Lucinda tell him something?"

"I don't believe so. I mean, maybe, but I doubt it. She went through so much shit when she got back from England. A unwed mother. No, I'm sure she didn't tell."

"How would you know that?"

"She wrote me. I got seven letters ovah the years before she died."

"But you said you can't read." I'm a detective, and a good detective knows that the first person he's got to investigate is his client.

"I don't know how to read. But Pinky do."

"Ernie's mother?"

"Yeah. She read the letters to me. Lu was careful. She talked about Chuck without sayin' he was ourn. But now that I think about it, she one time said that she told Chuck that his father was a man different from all the other men he ever known. An' when he tried to get more, she said that one day, if he had a daughter, she'd be able to tell him the truth on her wedding day."

"Damn," I said. "He's been waiting for you. He had no idea, but it had to be something that even his mother kept from him."

"Now him an' his girl have dropped outta sight. She stopped goin' to work at her architecture job, and he haven't gone to his office at all."

"And he probably has a dozen men looking for you and Lamont with pictures from video cameras."

"I messed up, Mr. McGill."

"And that's why you need me to deliver the letter to Justine before she says *I do*."

"That's it in a nutshell."

"The internet says the wedding is in two weeks. On the one hand, it's just passing a note. On the other, it means negotiating a wall of fire without getting burned." I stopped there to consider the depth of the job. Then: "Tell me one thing, Catfish."

"What's that?"

"If you planned to do this all on your own, then why would you even need to bring along Ernie's whiskey?"

"Pinky made me take it. She knew 'bout the letter. She knew they was rich. And one thing a poor sharecropper understands is that messin' with rich white people is like tipplin' poison. She gimme the whiskey and told me what to say jest in case we got in trouble."

"Well," I said. "If I want to survive to drink my whiskey, I guess I'll have to do my best."

"Is your best good enough?"

"Usually it is."

"I'M GONE AFTER THAT rabbit," Lamont sang behind a driving blues progression on his guitar, *"but she don't wan' none'a me."*

He played a few chords.

"I'm gone after that rabbit," Twill continued. I had no idea that my favorite son had such a pure voice in him. *"She don't want none'a me."*

Lamont grinned and strummed a while.

"They wanna pull my long hair," Mardi added in a voice that was from another day, another time, *"drag me down in infamy."*

Then the young people broke out in laughter. Catfish walked in among them, slapping his hands together.

It was at that moment I became committed to Catfish's cause. It felt as if they'd set music free in the world and, like some invisible alien god, that music was moving us, men and women, to a higher plane.

"Twill."

"Yeah, Pops?"

"Why don't you take Catfish and Lamont over to Gordo's."

Mardi pouted and gave a cute grunt to tell anyone who was interested that she was having fun and didn't want to lose her newfound friends so soon.

"Tell Gordo," I continued, "that I would appreciate it very much if he would put our friends up for the next two weeks."

"You got it," Twill said with authority. He was a throwback to a time when young people became adults before the law allowed them to drink.

"We got our things in a little hotel up in East Harlem," Catfish insisted.

"Anything you really need?" I asked.

"Everything I own."

"You could call and have them put it all in storage," I suggested.

"That's my private property, Mr. McGill."

"So's your life, Catfish."

"How they gonna know we up in some fleabag in Harlem? No, man, we'll go to the new place after we get our stuff."

I nodded out a few beats to my own internal blues, then said, "Okay. You'd be better not going back there, but all right. Go with Twill and pick up your stuff. But you got to remember—if a man as rich as Sternman is looking for you, you have to make your footprint as small as possible."

Catfish squinted in my direction and bobbed his head in understanding.

"I was after this buck one time in the fall down Mississippi," he said. "I swear at times it felt like that deer must'a sprouted wings to get away."

"You get him?"

"Not that year. But three seasons later, I come up on 'im in a clearin'. I knew it was him because he had this big black patch on his left haunch. I raised my rifle from behind these bushes. He lifted up his head, but he was only suspicious. I had my finger on the trigger, but I couldn't shoot. I jest stood there an' watched him till he finally wandered off."

"I doubt if your son will give you the same consideration."

"I'll go with you," Mardi said to Twill. "Maybe I can help."

AN HOUR AND FIFTEEN minutes later, I was on the fourteenth floor of a brick office building near Seventy-Second and Broadway. Halfway down the hall, I was assailed by the concussions of a relentless hip-hop beat emanating from the door to my destination. The stenciled words on the oak door read STICKS AND STONES SECURITY SERVICES (SSSS). I pressed a pink button to the right of the door, and the music instantly cut off. A few seconds later, the door swung inward, revealing the short and extremely well-formed Foxy Donk.

The black-skinned, cherry-red-headed young woman most often maintained a perpetual sneer, daring anyone to challenge her. But when she saw me, she grinned like she must have when she was a child and her father had just come home from work.

"Hey, Mr. McGill," she said, and then she hugged me.

A sweet smell arose from those bright red extensions, and the warmth her body exuded was enough to make a less focused man forget his purpose.

"Hey, Foxy," I said. "How you doin'?"

"Kissin' frogs and dodgin' bullets," she said, letting go and taking half a step backward.

I laughed, and her smile deepened.

"Wolfman here?" I inquired.

"Wolfie!" she shouted to nonexistent bleachers.

From a long hallway behind her desk, a deep voice bellowed, "What?"

"Don't you 'What?' me! Mr. McGill out here."

The heavy steps down the long hallway were familiar, like a giant's progress in a child's nightmare. When he emerged, I was impressed, as always, at Wolfman Chord's dimensions and strength. Six six, he weighed just south of 350 pounds. And if any of that was fat, only his lovers would know it. Wolfman's skin was a deep brass brown, and his face was that of an intelligent, inquisitive child. His biceps were round and hard under a bright blue sports jacket, and the diamond embedded in his left earlobe weighed at least four carats.

A few years earlier, Chord's accountant, Lothario Moran, a bespectacled black man from Baltimore, had somehow fixed the security expert's books so that it looked like he was stealing from his own company. Mr. Chord had come to me to find the fancified accountant so that he could kill him. I explained that even if he managed to kill Moran without getting caught, he'd still be in deep trouble over the embezzlement charges. I got my own CPA, Ernst Kahn, once a Geneva banker, to untangle the fabrications of Lothario. Ernst did a magnificent job. I turned this information over to Carson Kittridge, the most honest cop in New York, and now Lothario is serving between a nickel and a dime at Attica.

"Leo-nid!" Wolfman shouted.

"Wolfman."

He pumped my hand and slapped my shoulder with such pure force that I automatically began to plan how I would fight him if we were ever to meet in the ring, or some back-alley brawl.

"What can I do for you, brother?" he announced.

"Take it back to your playroom and hear me out."

The big baby face took on a canny expression and then smiled like a benevolent, deified moon. He turned and I made to follow, but before I could, Ms. Donk touched my arm.

"Drop by and say hello before you go, baby," she said.

I nodded, then took half a dozen quick steps to catch up to her boss.

THE PASSAGEWAY LEADING FROM Foxy's receptionist's area was unadorned and narrow, topped off by a low ceiling. It was more like a tunnel in a coal mine than a foyer on the fourteenth floor of a Manhattan office building. We had to walk single file, also like miners. Behind me, Foxy's hip-hop cranked up again. After maybe a dozen steps, that sound began to morph into something that sounded like Bach. Another dozen steps and we had made it to Wolfman's den, what someone might have called an office if they didn't mind using the term loosely.

The room was quite large, its ceiling a good nine feet higher than that of the connecting hall. The floor was laid with bright and shiny tiles that contained every color of the rainbow. There was a huge plasma TV on one wall that played, in equal quarters, four of the major cable news providers. The volume of the TV was muted so as not to interfere with the classical piece being played. There was no desk, just a matching sofa and chair upholstered in something like elephant skin, though I'm sure it was synthetic. The den also sported a full-size refrigerator, a counter with sink and cupboards, a white table that sat four, and a billiards table that I knew could be converted for Ping-Pong.

"What's this you got playin', man?" I asked.

"Processional Suite in C by Johann Joseph Fux."

"Fucks?"

"Yeah. F-U-X, Fux."

"Damn."

"You want sumpin' to drink?" the minor giant asked.

"I already had my drink for the day."

"Well then, come on over to my table an' tell me what you need."

I sat, and the music changed to a piece featuring flute and oboe. I don't know what the composition was for, but I imagined ballet dancers out on that mostly bare multicolored floor. Then the ample body of my host blocked out the ghostly pirouettes.

"You into the Sternman wedding?" I asked.

"Why?"

"I need to be on the security staff."

Wolfman stared at me like the supernatural predator he was named for. He tapped the nail of his right middle finger on the white enamel tabletop, not saying anything. I didn't speak, because I'd already made my request and that was all I was willing to reveal.

In this way our silences spoke to each other.

"Antonio Alberghetti got that job," Wolfman said at last. "He called me six weeks ago to see if I had any guys he could use."

"And did you?"

"This here is my bread and butter you stickin' your dirty fingers into, Leonid."

"If I didn't step in when Markham Peters put a target on your ass, somebody else be eatin' that greasy sandwich right now."

It wasn't only the accountant Wolfman owed me for. Two years earlier, Foxy Donk had come to me because she heard from a boyfriend who worked for Peters, a local gangster, that his boss had put up seventy-five hundred dollars to kill her boss. Wolfman had been doing body-guard work for a Hong Kong businessman named Féng. Markham's son, Jesse, took a dislike to Féng. Wolfman found it necessary to slap Jesse, and somehow the kid ended up with a broken ankle. I asked my good friend Hush to drop by Markham's and ask him to pay a kill fee on the hit. I do not believe that there is a man still living who ever said no to Hush—except me, of course.

"I know all that, Lee," Wolfman said. "But Millie's pregnant again and Foxy wanna raise. It's taken me years to make my contacts."

"I know. And I wish I could tell you that there won't

be any blowback, but I can't say that, either. All I know is that any trouble you get into, I'll be right there with you."

The music changed again. This time it was an organ sonata by Bach that I recognized but could not name.

"Lonnie Rudolf was the only guy of mine that Alberghetti was interested in," the security expert relented. Blood debts are hard to ignore.

"Can you ask Lonnie to step aside for me?"

"I can ask."

"Tell him he'll still get his money. I already got a client."

"Who's that?"

I smiled and stood.

"You see yourself out?" he asked.

"Foxy wants to tell me something anyway."

"Okay. I'll call Lonnie and see what he has to say."

"They call him Two Times, right?"

"Yeah. Got that from one'a his girlfriends, I forget her name. She used to say, 'If you cain't do two times you better off leaving Lonnie alone.'"

FOXY WAS WORKING ON her nails when I lowered into a chair beside her desk. She turned down the music but continued working on the baby fingernail of her left hand.

"How are you, girl?"

"When you gonna call me?"

Foxy's thirty-first birthday fell six weeks before. I knew this because she invited me through an email service. I hadn't come but sent flowers. This because I was so much closer to sixty than I was to thirty-one.

"You know there are people who would like to see me in jail for even entertaining the thought of being out on a date with you," I said.

"So?" Her eyes and warmth and posture were more dangerous than the pistol in my pocket.

"Gimme a break, will ya, Foxy? You know what you got there. And you see me tryin' to hold back."

"I don't want no gold ring or no kids," she declared. "I just want a real man up in my life—at least one time."

I wanted to say no. I certainly should have said no. But through my veins flows the blood of humanity, and that genetic code knows only yes and death.

But thankfully, due to my father homeschooling me on Freud, I had learned how to put off gratification.

"Let me think on that for a while," I said. "I'll call you soon and say what I can."

Foxy Donk sneered at me, exhibiting real satisfaction. I believe that she was temporarily sated by my hesitation. I stood up, and she smiled for me.

"I'll be seein' you soon, Leonid."

"Yes, baby," I dutifully replied . . . and then I was gone.

*   *   *

ON THE STREET AGAIN, I was feeling pretty good about myself. I knew Lonnie Rudolf. He'd step aside from the security job if Wolfman asked him to. All I had to do was let him collect the check, and I'd be right next to the bride-to-be. That done, I'd cancel my debt to Ernie Eckles, save the bluesman whose great-great-grandson showed me that my son could sing, and earn a mason jar full of the best whiskey I'd ever tasted.

Pleased, I took out my phone.

There were three texts from Mardi and one from Twill. Mardi's texts were all in caps and red.

HE'S BEEN SHOT MR. M! HE'S BEEN SHOT!

HE'S NOT DEAD. LAMONT IS PUTTING PRESSURE ON THE WOUND AND TWILL WENT AFTER THE SHOOTERS.

I TEXTED RAINIER'S CLINIC. SHE CALLED BACK AND SAID THAT THERE'S AN AMBULANCE ON THE WAY.

All things considered, I was impressed with Mardi's focus under duress. The fourth text was from Twill.

photograph of the license plate attached. i hit back but
they got away. maybe pink maybe not. we're in the ambulance on the way to Rainier's

That was a lot to process. My ninety-four-year-old
client had been shot. Even if they only grazed a finger,
he could go into shock and die. Somehow the people
working for my client's son had found him. Hopefully it
was at the Harlem hotel. But still…an ambulance could
be traced. The worst revelation was that Twill had gone
armed and had possibly wounded one of the hit men.
That's what *hit back* and *pink* meant. But all that would
have to wait. I composed a text, sent it, and then started
walking—fast. Rainier's was on the West Side near Sixty-
Eighth, so I'd make it in twelve minutes or less.

WHEN I TOOK ON the case, not three hours earlier,
it was about young people, good music, even better
whiskey, and a letter for a young woman that said
something she needed to know—or not. Now it was
blood and tears, bullets and possibly prison time for
my son. Goddamn.

RAINIER'S CLINIC OCCUPIED THE fifth floor of the five-
story Brown Medical Building. Brown's was made from

dark red brick and tenanted by plastic surgeons, ortho-pedists, blood-work and X-ray laboratories, and one bone specialist. The private elevator that connected the street to Rainier's exclusive emergency room was large enough to carry six gurneys and twice that many paramedics. This lift brought me to the receptionist's desk. Tiny, at least partly Asian, and ageless, the daytime admissions officer, Agnes Smalls, sat at her usual post. Next to her stood Lana Rainier.

Lana was a year or two older than I, though she looked about a decade younger. She usually wore a white lab coat over a muted pantsuit, with her ample gray-and-brown hair tied up into a bun at the back of her head. She'd held the position of head physician in a series of city emer-gency rooms over the past twenty-one years.

At some point along the way, Lana got addicted to heroin. Not opioids with fancy Latin names but smack, black tar, the kind of poison you could once buy in little plastic bags from Hell's Kitchen to Times Square, from the East Village to Brownsville.

Lana's habit had been found out by her last hospital's night supervisor, Sherman Wale. It was Wale's intention to report her to the police. He would have done just that if it wasn't for the hospital policy that all dealings with the police had to go through the security office. Sitting at the nighttime receiving desk of this office was Plymouth Crews. Lana had saved Plymouth's mother's life when she was brought in suffering from a severe infarction. Plymouth called Lana to tell her about what the night supervisor wanted him to do. Lana called a mid-level thug named Dexter Lewis. Dexter offered to have the night supervisor severely beaten, but Lana demurred.

That's when I was called in.

Sherman Wale could have been canonized in his lifetime. He had never stolen, lied, or knowingly caused injury to another human being. He was almost exactly my color and never missed a Sunday at Loving Episcopal. He cared for his aging mother in his own home, believed in honesty, was the soul of honesty, and so I decided, without approaching him, that he could not be moved.

The next morning, I set up a meeting with the head of the hospital, a woman named Gillis.

"If you let Dr. Rainier go without police involvement, I can assure you that there will be no nosy journalists looking for more skeletons in your closets," I said after laying out the problem Sherman Wale represented.

Gillis was a short woman with bobbed gray hair and rubber-soled, sensible brown shoes.

"No need for threats, Mr. McGill," she said. "Dr. Rainier

is the best emergency room doctor we've ever had. She not only saves lives but afterwards keeps in touch with the patients while they're recovering. No. I do not want her reported to the police any more than you do. I wish Sherman had come to me. I certainly don't care what she's had to do to self-medicate with all the suffering and death she's seen."

AFTER THE NEGOTIATIONS WERE over, I connected Dr. Rainier with a group of investors who knew a good thing when they saw it. They put up serious money for her to establish her own private emergency clinic on Sixty-Eighth. Adding the doctor's considerable expertise, well-trained staff, and a certain level of discretion she had about reporting the nature of patients' wounds, Rainier was able to develop a thriving, if not quite kosher, business.

As an extra added benefit, she took care of me and mine any time of the day or night.

"WHAT THE HELL IS wrong with you, McGill?" were the good doctor's first words to me on the day Catfish Worry was shot. "You're so hard that you put a ninety-year-old man and three children in jeopardy?"

"Good to know what you think'a me, Doc. I mean,

you asked the right question, but it doesn't seem like you need any answers."

"That man is here," she said in a tone full of dread and threat.

"We'll talk about that, but first I wanna know how Catfish is doing."

Lana took a moment to recalibrate her thoughts and emotions.

"Yes," she said. "Of course. He was shot in the left shoulder with a small-caliber bullet. He didn't bleed much because pressure was applied immediately. One of my ex-military surgeons has already removed the bullet."

"What's the prognosis?"

"No extreme physical trauma. No shock. He asked for whiskey to calm his nerves. I gave him some of mine." She smiled. "He made one young nurse blush by just looking at her."

I sighed in relief. "Thank you, Lana. Believe me when I tell you this man's troubles started before he ever met me. He came to my office less than four hours ago, and I tried to talk him out of going to that hotel. When can he be moved?"

"I'd like to keep him for observation overnight."

"That's good conservative procedure, Doctor, but the

ambulance that brought him here can be traced, and, believe me, you don't want that kind of fallout."

Lana Rainier winced, and then her jaw clenched. She had a long face that was somehow both doughy and elegant.

"I'm doing the same thing for him that I did for you," I assured her. "There's no malice here."

Slowly the doctor's facial tension eased.

"I know that," she said. "It's just that you cut it so close to the bone."

"No different than you. Now, where'd you put *that man*?"

MY CLAN WERE THE only ones occupying the blue waiting room. The emergency clinic maintained six waiting rooms, coded by a child's color wheel.

Mardi was sitting close to Lamont, steadily whispering words of hope and support. In the opposite corner, Twill was speaking more openly to my friend Hush— ex-assassin extraordinaire.

I went over to Lamont and Mardi. They were so concentrated on each other that they didn't notice me at first. I placed a hand on the young man's shoulder, and he stood right up.

"Mr. McGill."

"Sit down. Sit down," I said. "The surgeon is finished.

If everything is all right, you and Catfish will go with that man over there talking to Twill."

I pulled up a chair.

"Who is he?"

"He'll take you to a safe place and stay there with you until I can clear things up."

"I'm sorry, Mr. McGill. You tried to warn us."

"I want to go with them," Mardi said. There's steel in that girl.

"No, honey." I placed my hand on hers. "I need you in the office. And once Hush places them, no one can know where they are. Not even you."

"Can he protect C-Paw?" Lamont wanted to know.

"Yes."

"We shouldn't'a gone to that hotel," the young man lamented. "All it was was some clothes an' guitar strings."

"Don't worry, Lamont. Nobody's dead."

I got up and went to the other corner to greet my friend and Twill.

"Hey, Pops," Twill greeted. He was smiling as always. As comfortable as a cat sitting in a sunlit window.

"You and I have to talk," I told him.

"I know. First we get Catfish settled, and then I'm all yours."

Talking to Twill was like playing a game of Go; words

were pieces that accrued on all sides until, in the end, victory was the child of sacrifice.

"You got the dimensions?" I asked the man known as Hush.

There was nothing exceptional about him. The professional killer was of medium height with a slight build and skin that Americans called white. He had brown eyes and hair. No, there was nothing to set him apart except that he could kill anyone, anywhere, with anything at all.

"Yeah," he said in his low rumble of a voice. "Very professional crew. You want me to go after 'em?"

"No. I promised Tamara that I wouldn't be the cause of you falling off that wagon. I just need you to salt my client away."

Hush gave me one of his rare smiles. He was retired, married, and a father. Killing haunted him, called to him, it was the only thing he had a passion for—before having a son.

"Okay. I'll keep 'em both safe, Leonid," Hush promised. "You can do the rest."

"Let's take a walk."

THE WALLS OF THE post-op room were the palest the color pink could be before giving in to white. Catfish Worry lay beneath white sheets up to his neck. The bluesman's head was nestled on a white pillow. Add all that to the container of opalescent walls, and his face shone like a black pearl.

"Sorry, Mr. McGill," he said.

"Water under the bridge," I assured him. "This is my friend Hush. Hush, this is Mr. Catfish Worry."

"Pleased to meet you," Hush said.

"You got dead eyes, brothah."

"They've seen a lot."

"Oh yeah? What they see in me?"

"He's going to take you someplace safe," I said by way of answering the question. "In the meantime, I'll get that letter to your granddaughter. If I can, I'll stop your son from trying anything else against you."

"He that good, Dead-eye?" Catfish asked Hush.

"Better'n most," my friend replied, falling easily into blues patter.

THINGS MOVED SMOOTHLY AFTER that, like a gurney gliding down a linoleum hallway carrying the condemned to that final appointment.

There was a secret way out of the Brown Medical Building. My entire tribe took the express elevator to the basement and then climbed some stairs through to an exit on Sixty-Seventh Street. Hush had one of the cars used for his limo company waiting to receive him, Catfish, and Lamont. Twill, Mardi, and I took the subway downtown.

We didn't talk on the ride. Mardi was sad over her new friends' suffering. I was angry at Twill for carrying a gun and at myself for not suspecting that he would.

We got to the Tesla Building and my offices in less than half an hour. Twill went on to the inner office space while Mardi took up her post as sentry. I stood for a moment before her desk, trying to gather my thoughts.

"I'm going to move you to the main space," I said after an overly long span of silence.

"You don't want me answering the door anymore?"

"You will, but we'll automate the lock so you can ring people in without putting yourself in jeopardy."

"Don't do that, Mr. McGill. The last thing I need is you thinking I'm too delicate to look after myself."

I heard the argument. Maybe I even agreed with it. As concerned as I might have been, I had no right to take away her freedom.

"You don't need to worry about Catfish," I said. "Lana says he's doing great, and I intend to do what he wants, then deal with the response."

"But would that get you in trouble?"

"To paraphrase the great Sugar Ray Robinson," I said, "trouble is what I do."

Mardi smiled for me and then turned on her computer.

I headed for the main office space and the most serious problem I had to face — my son.

"Hey," he said when I stopped at his post. There was a picture of Charles Sternman on his computer screen. Our tech expert, Bug Bateman, had equipped us with a search engine that made Google seem like a covered wagon carrying a meager carton of books.

I settled my bulk on the edge of his desk and asked, "What's wrong with you, son?"

"I only carry when I think there might be a problem, Pops." Twill gave a slight shrug with his left shoulder.

"Picking up a suitcase from a Harlem hotel sounded like a problem to you?"

"It was Mardi," Twill countered, holding up his palms like the span between two steps on a staircase. "When she pays that much attention to somebody, it means there's somethin' up. And Lamont was actin' funny too."

"How would you know that? You just met Lamont."

"It's the way he kept lookin' up at the door, like he was expecting trouble."

"Let me ask you a question," I said.

"Shoot."

"When I sent you to that pool hall where Jordi Hooper's heist gang met, did you go there armed?"

"Course not. If they found out, they would'a tried to hurt me. If I pulled on them, they would'a killed me. And even if they didn't, I wouldn't have gotten what you sent me there to get. Uh-uh, Pops. Between Mardi bein' so friendly, Lamont bein' so nervous, and you sendin' them to Uncle Gordo—I knew somethin' was up."

Being the father of a criminal genius like Twill is no easy task. He loves me, wants my approval. But when it comes to the life he lives day to day—that will always be conducted according to his real-time discretion.

"I'll tell you what," I said. "If you ever get the feeling that you need to go armed, working for me or not, tell me about it first. Whether you're on the job or just going to some party—tell me first."

The beautiful young man mulled the request over just behind his eyes. This wasn't rudeness, but that Twilliam is a thinker as well as a troublemaker.

"You got it, Pops," he said after a hundred seconds or so.

I sighed and then pulled up one of his phantom co-workers' chairs to see what his advanced search parameters revealed.

MAYBE HALF AN HOUR later, his intercom spoke.

"Twill?"

"Yeah, Mar?"

"Do you know where your father is? I can't reach him."

"What is it, Mardi?" I called.

"Captain Kittridge," a decidedly masculine voice replied.

"Come on down, Kit," I said, betraying little to none of the trepidation I felt. "I'll be in my office."

I WAS ALREADY SEATED with my back to Lower Manhattan when Captain Carson Kittridge came through the doorway. Kit is even shorter than I, at five five even. We stand eye to eye, but in every other way, we're opposites. He's the color of bleached bone and slender enough to be a teenager. As far as I knew, Kit had never broken a law in his life; he rarely bruised a rule. People who are so virtuous usually tend toward vengeance rather than forgiveness.

"Captain."

"What's this license plate you sent to Officer Broadman?" Another quirk of Kit's personality was that he had no manners.

"If I'm not mistaken," I said, "I sent that text to Benny's private cell. Isn't it a breach of a man's civil rights to monitor his private communications?"

"Cops have no privacy." Kit lowered into a client's chair.

"I'm not a cop."

"I wasn't talking about you."

"You are if you read my communiqué."

That assertion stopped the righteous cop for a beat or two.

"Tell me what you want with Sal Peretti," Kit demanded.

"Never heard of the man," I lied.

"You didn't know the plate you sent belongs to Peretti's aunt in Paramus?"

"What do you want, Kit?"

"Peace on earth and your ass in prison. And, while we're at it, what the hell is Twill doing here?"

"Like father, like son."

Yet another difference between us was that I honestly liked Kit. He's smart and dogged, a worthy opponent in an undeserving world. Like any good adversary, in or out of the ring, he sought my downfall while I struggled to stay on my feet.

"There was a shootout at the Holton Hotel up in Harlem earlier today," he said.

"There was a flood in Sudan and probably an earthquake on Mars. What the fuck does any of that have to do with me?"

"A white guy fired the first shots," Kit explained. "A slender young African American male returned fire."

"Lots of angry young black men in New York," I said. "Most of them, however, are unemployed. My skinny-assed son spends his days working at that desk where you passed him."

The honest cop drew in a deep breath.

"Look, man," I said. "I know you been mad that the brass had you shut down surveillance on my activities. I know we'll never be friends, but why don't you relax for a minute and have a drink with me? I just got hold of some good whiskey."

Kit took four, maybe five long breaths before saying, "You got everybody fooled, don't you, L.T.? Maybe you even believe the bullshit yourself...."

I wondered for a moment if the constant cop was aware of the depth of his own question. I shrugged.

That was the hardheaded captain's cue to stand.

"You might have convinced Garrity that you're no longer a threat, but that doesn't matter to me. I don't need a surveillance crew to keep tabs on you. I got the one piece of information I'll ever need to put you away for good."

"Oh? And what might that be?" I really was curious.

"As slick as any crook is," he said, "one day he's bound to slip up."

Captain Carson Kittridge turned on his heel and stalked out of my aerie.

I don't believe he understood that his perpetual watch over my every step was one of the things that kept me sharp.

After I saw Kit exit Mardi's office through my surveillance monitor, I punched in Twill's extension on the intercom and said, "Get your things together. We're going to put a little surveillance on a man named Peretti."

"Sal Peretti?"

"The same."

"Heavy?" he asked over the line.

"No."

SAL PERETTI SPENT HIS evenings making the rounds of brothels, illicit nightclubs, gambling establishments, and those places where people like Lana Rainier might procure drugs. He was the bagman for various bosses and known for his ability to deliver.

At night, he was a man on the move.

But most afternoons, Sal could be found at Derby's Men's Club near a nameless alley adjacent to the Brooklyn Navy Yard. When he was younger, Sal's betters belonged to a club that was exclusively Italian and housed in Little Italy. But as time has passed, Peretti and his generation have had to settle for a multicultural Caucasian fraternity, an association much like colonial America, when all the different tribes of Europe agreed that they were white people—whatever that meant.

I rented an outer-borough green cab from a friend of mine. Twill parked the taxi two blocks away, shooing off potential customers by telling them his car had been leased as a limo by a guy from Turkey.

There was a small bodega across the street from Derby's. Dressed in my ripest rags, I installed myself on the curb in front of that little store. There I begged for change and offered to help people with anything from opening the door to giving directions. Festooned in a red bandanna, I wore a Korean War army surplus jacket and jeans stained and stiff enough that they could stand on their own.

I'd placed a beer-can camera lens at the bottom of a city-supplied wire garbage can. The lens transmitted a streaming image of the front of Derby's Men's Club to Twill's computer screen.

On the whole, it was a fruitful afternoon. The weather was pleasant, so Sal sat at an outside table drinking something from a coffee cup and shooting the shit with other club members.

"WHAT ARE YOU DOING here?" someone asked my back when I had just helped an old woman lift her wheeled shopping cart down three steps from the bodega entrance.

The question was official-sounding, so I pocketed the dollar tip, turned, and said, "Afternoon, Officers."

There were two of them standing in a flanking position from which they could easily keep me from running or striking out with some concealed weapon. I didn't hold that against them. A cop's beat is hostile territory on the best days.

One uniform had red hair and a child's innocent face. The other patrolman had bloodshot eyes. They were both white and under the age of thirty. This last detail was important because younger cops tended not to recognize me.

"Time to move on," the bloodshot cop said. I decided to think of him as Player.

"You heard him, Pops," his partner added. "Let's go."

I named the redhead cop Joker because I found it humorous that he called me by the same endearment Twill used.

"But, Officers." I infused my words with a plaintive tone. "I been given permission to stand here an' help my fellow man."

I grinned and saw out of the corner of my eye a man with his arm in a sling had stopped to talk with Peretti. I wanted to get a better look, but that might have exposed me to discovery.

"Don't think we won't take you into that alley and bust your head," Player was saying.

"...like eggplant target practice on Ku Klux Day in June," Joker said, finishing the threat.

It was almost too much information. Player was a bad cop and Joker was worse. Also, I suspected that Joker, despite his red hair, had some Italian in him—because of the eggplant slur. The greatest danger was that these guys were a well-oiled team—finishing each other's sentences, escalating their threat word by word.

But I had a trick up my tattered sleeve. Flexing the ring and middle fingers of my left hand, like Spider-Man shooting his web, I pincered a card kept in the cuff of my army jacket sleeve. This I proffered for the boy-men to see.

"What's that?" red-eyed Player asked.

"Ma gooj," I replied with a grin.

This particular *get out of jail free* card, sometimes known as a gooj, was given to me by Art Garrity, one of the most highly ranked cops in the NYPD. Even Aryan Brotherhood goose-steppers like Joker had to stop and pay heed to that ticket.

"Is that what I think it is?" Player asked his partner.

"I'll call it in," the redhead replied, plucking the card from my fingers. "Probably just found it dumpster diving."

Joker walked a few yards away to make a call on his cell phone.

SOME MONTHS BEFORE, ART Garrity's son Nicholas had been kidnapped by an anarchist group calling themselves the People's Revolutionary Orgy. PRO demanded the release of thirty-six political prisoners being held on Rikers Island. The nineteen-year-old already had a pinky removed and delivered to One Police Plaza for what they called *proof of purchase.*

When chasing down capitalist criminals, I follow the money as tradition demands. But for anarchists and other political extremists, I find it useful to step outside the box. The best radical detective in the world is a man who goes by the name Archibald Lawless.

Lawless is a modern-day acolyte of Mikhail Bakunin and Emma Goldman. He doesn't take money, and he rarely works for the cops. But if you can convince him that any dissident group is using a political excuse for criminal activity, he might decide to help. To that end, I entered a code on a mostly unknown entity called the Chartreuse Web....

"Hello," he said.

"Leonid here, Archibald."

"Mr. Detective. What brings you to my dacha?"

I explained the situation, being very careful not to lie or even mildly exaggerate any facts.

"Are you being paid for this job?" Archibald asked.

"It's a favor for the boy's father—Art Garrity."

There was a moment of silence. If Lawless didn't like the request, he would simply disengage the connection. If he thought I was lying, he'd cancel my code.

"There's a man who runs a pickpocket ring at Penn Station," the professional anarchist said.

"Billy Wrongman," I said. "He's the one wears a velvet jacket with the letters N-I-L embossed on the back."

"That's your man."

BILLY TOLD ME THAT the leader of the PRO was a woman named Mozelle Tot. Among other things, she was a serious opium smoker. That being such a rarefied addiction, it was the easiest thing in the world for me track her down and follow her to the Queens warehouse where Nicholas was being held.

Mr. Garrity loved his son as much as I did Twill. So he quashed Kit's ongoing reconnaissance of my movements and gave me a gooj that would get me out of any jam short of political assassination.

*   *   *

WHEN JOKER GOT BACK to us, he was no longer smiling. He walked right up to my face, nearly quivering with rage. Then, with an act of pure will, he handed the card back to me.

"Is there," he said, and then he paused. "Is there anything we can do for you, sir?"

Player was astonished. I glanced over at the guys in front of Derby's. They were wondering about us too.

"Put the cuffs on me and take me to your car," I said as if I was a major and he a private. "Drive me six blocks away and then let me out."

"You want us to make it rough?" Joker asked, I thought a little hopefully.

"Not if you want to hold on to your shield, son."

"What's goin' on?" Player whined.

"Just put the cuffs on him, George. Let's get the fuck outta here."

"WHERE YOU COMIN' FROM, Pops?" Twill asked when I finally made it back to the green cab. "I couldn't see you at all through the lens there for a while."

I explained what happened.

"Damn, Dad," he said with a chuckle. "Like the man says, 'If it wasn't for bad luck...'"

"What about the guy in the sling?"

"That's the dude I shot. Looks like I got him in the same place he hit Mr. Worry. I guess karma really is a bitch."

I DECIDED TO STAY in the taxi with Twill. We saw Sal head out from Derby's a few minutes shy of four. A car from Starzine Motorcoach and Limo Service picked him up, so we didn't have much time. The beer-can camera cost me thirty-five hundred dollars, but I just had to hope no one was pulling recyclables out in the neighborhood that evening.

I took the wheel.

Half the way across the Manhattan Bridge, Twill gave a whoop and holler.

"What?" I asked.

Looking at the computer screen, he said, "I just got into the Starzine GPS tracking system. The car Peretti's in is number one twenty-seven. We could track him from here to Inner Mongolia."

THAT NIGHT WE TOOK an excursion of all the five boroughs. Sal went to clubs and drug dens and restaurants— all leading to an assignation with a young Asian woman with bright blue hair. I supposed that Sal's deal with the girl's pimp was that he got to get it on with her now and then.

They went down a dimly lit alley in Flushing about 11:45. She led him to a doorway and went in first as he looked around to make sure they were alone.

The shadow my son and I had chosen to hide in was proof against the bagman's night vision.

They were gone for five minutes, more than enough time for Twill and me to construct a flexible plan.

There were four possible scenarios, the most likely of which was Sal coming out first. Two had Blue Hair in the lead, and, least likely, three was them coming out arm in arm. The wild card was Sal leaving by another exit, but that was okay because we could still track his limo via GPS.

The bagman proved predictable. When he stepped out of the doorway, I sucker punched him and kicked the door shut on the girl. Twill wedged a metal garbage can under the doorknob.

After applying handcuffs and a passable gag, we wrangled the unconscious gangster into the trunk of the cab and headed for an office building I knew on the East Side of Upper Midtown Manhattan.

*　　*　　*

SAL DIDN'T COME TO until after he'd been chained to a bronze chair in a one-room subbasement that only I had access to.

"What is this shit?" The left side of Sal's jaw had blown up to twice its normal size. I suspected he was in serious pain.

I kept quiet while he looked around. Part of my interrogation technique was the circumstances into which he'd been placed. The floor was concrete and cold. The walls were pale green with foamy white corrosion here and there. It was only me and him and a bare forty-watt lightbulb. I'd sent Twill to pick up the beer-can camera and then go home to tell his mother and my father that I'd be working all night.

HALF MY CHILDHOOD ALL the way into my fifties, I thought my father had died in Chile while fighting for the worldwide revolution. For forty years he'd been dead. Then he showed up in New York and moved in with me and my family. He promised that everything was different now, that he only wanted to be there for his grandchildren like he wasn't for me and Nikita, my brother.

He'd promised my mother that he'd be home from South America in eighteen months. While waiting, she died of a broken heart.

*   *   *

"ARE YOU CRAZY?" SAL Peretti asked.

"That's a good question. They say a man suffering from severe mental illness is often ill-equipped to assess that state of mind."

"I'll kill you," Sal vowed.

The sallow-faced thug yanked furiously at his chains. His breathing became erratic.

"Lemme up from here!" He tried to keep the plea tone out of his voice, but the fear of death is a close relative to truth.

The swelling in Sal's jaw was slowly closing his left eye.

"What?" he asked after almost two full minutes of struggle and failure.

"Who's the guy with his arm in a sling?"

The left eye shut completely. A clear viscous liquid oozed from the fold of flesh.

"You know what'll happen if I don't show up for my boss at the end of the night?" He tried his best to make the question sound threatening.

"Probably wonder where the twenty-four thousand seven hundred twenty-two dollars went," I said. "Then, after a few months, people'll be asking, 'Whatever happened to Sal Peretti?' Then . . . nothing."

Nothingness. That's the big fear of all creatures. To be blotted out of existence, facedown and floating in the river Styx.

"Bernard Shefly," Sal said in a state of complete moral defeat.

I raised my eyebrows and tilted my head to the side, telling his one good eye that I needed him to fill in the blanks.

"I don't know," he replied. "Said he needed to find this old nigger…Afro-American…He told me he needed to find this African American guy, all right? And I, I took him there."

"How would you know where he was?"

"I asked a cop I'm friendly with to do a hotel registration search for a man named Worry. You know—since anti-terrorism, the cops know how many peanuts in your shit. Anyway, Shefly didn't tell me he was gonna shoot the guy."

"Okay. I already know what he looks like. Now all I need is a location."

Crooks hate snitching the way aging beauty hates the mirror; it's an act that is both humiliating and, ultimately, unavoidable.

"He eats at Mama So's every afternoon."

"That's all?" I asked.

"What the fuck else do you want?"

"It's not what I want, Sal. It's what you need."

"Fuck you, man! What's that even supposed to mean?"

"It means that I'm gonna leave you down here while I check this guy out. It means if I get slaughtered leaving Mama's, no one will know where you are."

It was an evil pleasure seeing Sal's left eye trying to open wide. He cut loose with a loud fart and yanked against his chains some more.

"I just know where he eats at," my prisoner whined, his rank fragrance filling the small torture room. "How'm I gonna know what kinda protection he got?"

I nodded, smiled, and then strolled toward the door. From there I saluted Sal. When I pulled the door open, he screamed for all he was worth. It didn't matter. That room was the only one in the subbasement—no sound could escape that crypt.

AT 5:00 A.M. I went to Gordo's eighth-floor gym. The scrawny nonagenarian watched me throw punches at the heavy bag for eighteen minutes or so.

"Go on up to your room and take a nap," he said when I began to falter—not even half the way through my regular routine.

Glancing his way, I saw two of him and thought that the one on the left was probably right.

*   *   *

A LITTLE MORE THAN a year earlier, Gordo came down
with a virulent strain of cancer. I took him home either to
live or to die. He lived, and afterward dedicated a simple
room to me a few floors above the gym. It was easy for
him to do, seeing that Gordo owned the entire midtown
office building.

I SLEPT LIKE THAT imagined corpse, floating in the river
of death, not dreaming or hoping or believing in anything; just a lump of flesh with ice water for blood.

I woke up at noon, conscious but not really refreshed.

At 1:30 I walked into a third-floor restaurant a few
blocks south and east of Broadway and Canal.

Mama So's is a need-to-know kind of place. You won't
find it on Yelp or Google. American Express can't book
you a reservation, and no credit card could cover the cost.
Many a man's fate had been sealed at the dozen or so
spindly-legged black-lacquered tables. More than a few
lives had been spared there, too.

A man in a light blue work shirt and dark blue trousers
was seated alone in a corner. His left arm hung in a
sling; he was deftly eating noodles with a pair of chop-
sticks using his unimpaired right hand. There were other

customers scattered around the dining room. Most of them looked up when I walked in. More than a few recognized me. No one waved. When I was an active crook, my presence was sought after, often as a last resort...but rarely was I welcome.

"Mr. McGill." The accent was cultured American English.

I turned and said, "Hello, Harry."

Harry Wong was somewhere between thirty and sixty with short black hair and an expression that was happy to see you come or go. He was born wearing that tuxedo, and his soul had been bartered away three generations before his birth.

"I don't have you in the book," Harry told me. It was a fact that was also a warning.

"Mr. Shefly and I have business to conduct."

"That is not in the book either."

"He's right over there," I observed. "Why not ask him?"

Wong was four inches taller and thirty pounds lighter than I. We were both dangerous men. He had no fear of conflict, but like any successful son of Darwin, he preferred the path of least resistance.

"Wait here," he said.

Harry asking Shefly the question was the most I could hope for. Mama So's was not a place you could force your way into. But even if the wounded gangster sent me away, he'd still know I was onto him. And if he didn't know who I was, Wong would serve up that information.

LOOKING AROUND THE ROOM, I found unbidden memories filling my mind. The recollection of past meetings disturbed me. I had done some bad things in my life: helped the worst criminals evade justice, sent men and women on that one-way trip down the river. Some of them never returned. They might have been guilty of other crimes but not the ones I set them up for. At one time I blamed my father's abandonment for these sins, but I had learned that in the end, wrong is wrong and every man has to carry his own water.

"Mr. Shefly would be happy for you to join him, Mr. McGill," Harry Wong said, and past sins took a back seat to my current revival.

"MR. SHEFLY," I SAID, standing over the man and his noodles.

"Have a seat, Mr. McGill."

I settled into the chair opposite, looking into the would-be killer's eyes. His chest, sculpted by weight lifting, was topped off with a ruggedly handsome face and hair that couldn't make up its mind between blond and brunette. His eyes were gray.

"Can I order you something to eat?" the gunman offered.

"Not just yet."

"Mr. Wong tells me that you used to be a regular around here," he said to break the silent stare.

"I was in a slightly different line of business in those days."

"What brings you around this afternoon?"

"I have entered an agreement to protect Catfish Worry."

"You got to me right quick," he said, plucking up a snow pea with his sticks. "You should really try these noodles, L.T."

He knew my reputation and why I was there and still showed no fear.

"I need to talk to the man that sent you up to Harlem yesterday. Can you give me his name?" I didn't expect any kind of direct answer, but I needed to ask before I acted.

"Hilton Zeal," Shefly said, and the room actually seemed to dim.

I'm known as a man who keeps his cool, but that name made me blink.

"You know him?" Shefly asked, doing a pretty good impression of Mona Lisa's smile.

"Since you're being so forthcoming," I said by way of answering, "maybe you can tell me where to find him."

Shefly popped another snow pea into his mouth and chewed on my question.

He swallowed and said, "I can't imagine you'd have anything to say to the man."

"Where you from, Bernard? I never heard of you."

"I came from Chi about a year or so ago."

"Then maybe you're not fully aware of my standing in our community. If I say I need to talk to somebody, then they need to talk to me."

Bernard put down his sticks and leveled that gray gaze at me.

"I'll tell him that," he said.

I'd gotten further than I'd expected but not the distance I had to go. Harry Wong was watching me from the entrance. There were probably a dozen other hidden eyes watching, waiting for my next move.

Adding those eyes to the name Hilton Zeal, I decided it was time to depart.

"Thank you, Mr. Shefly," I said, rising to my feet. "You've been quite helpful."

He nodded, gesturing that he didn't want to speak through a mouthful of noodles.

*   *   *

"YOU SHOULD CALL THE next time," Harry said to my back as I went out the door.

I didn't answer him.

"HILTON ZEAL," HUSH SAID.

Hush, Catfish, Lamont, and I were sitting around a coffee table in the four-bedroom apartment the ex-assassin kept over Pruitt's Drugs and Sundries in Nyack.

"Who's Hilton Zee?" Catfish asked.

"He's considered the most dangerous criminal on the East Coast by law enforcement," Hush said. "And quite a few on the other side of the line agree with that assessment. He's only about fifty but old-school and slick as shit in olive oil."

"You know him?" Lamont asked me.

"Only by reputation. I'm sure he knows me the same way."

"So why's he after me?" Catfish asked.

"Zeal's an upscale crook," I replied. "Rich people come to him because they believe he's more reliable than those further down the line. You know, people like me. Odds are your son hired him."

"So what you sayin'?" Catfish wanted to know.

"The safest thing to do would be for you two to drop the whole thing and go back to Mississippi," Hush advised.

"But," I added, "if you still want to move ahead, it'd be best to try and convince your son to back off."

"And if he refuses," Hush said, finishing the round, "maybe we should make him die."

"No," Catfish asserted. "He's my son. I don't even know for a fact that he hired this Zee."

Worry was adamant, and he was the client. And things weren't as bad as Hush made them sound. But even if he was right—the good thing about being between a rock and a hard place was that you don't have much of a choice.

"How's the shoulder, Mr. Worry?" I asked.

"Kinda stiff," he said. "That lady doctor said it was a twenty-two caliber. You know I still got muscle up in that shoulder from my cotton-pickin' days." It was almost as if he were putting together his next blues song. "You got a answer for this tangle, Mr. McGill?"

"Maybe. I'll need a little more information from you, but I already know how to get to your granddaughter."

We talked for a little while after that, and then I took the 516 bus back to Manhattan.

*　　*　　*

MY ANARCHIST FATHER AND chaotic wife had dinner with Twill and me almost every night over the next week. Katrina was very nice and loving to me—always a bad sign. In between domestic festivities, I planned the two-pronged attack on Charles Sternman and his unsuspecting daughter.

I'd sent Mardi and her younger sister to stay with Hush and spent most days at home in my den making calls; now and then I went out on errands or for sessions at the gym.

We were eating dinner about a week before the Sternman wedding. That evening my father talked about the politics of gender and the megacapitalist cultures playing geographic and ecologic roulette, the fallacy of what he called DNA-derived identity and how the wick of capitalism was destined to sputter and go out.

"Speaking of capitalism," I said, "what are you doing for money?"

"Leonid," Katrina chided.

"That's all right, Kat," my father said with aplomb. My father is a hale man, tall and charismatic. "He's right. I can't live on your charity forever. I mean, I was on the front lines of the revolution in Asia, Africa, and South

America, too. But they don't have retirement plans for insurrectionists. Every man and woman, boy and girl, domesticated animal and wild beast, must contribute to their survival or die."

"I know a few folks could use a competent explosives expert," I offered.

"Leonid," was Katrina's reply to my impudence. "Your father was . . . he is a hero."

"Not to me and my brother. Not to our mother, who's no more than dust and bones somewhere out there in a potter's field."

Even then, I knew that I wasn't angry at my father, not really. Just like Johnny Cash's boy named Sue, I had been made strong by his gift of travails. No, what bothered me was the complexity and dangers posed by the case at hand. Charles Sternman was the billionaire son of a poor man he wished dead. I had put my body in the way and so made myself, and my son, potential casualties. Then there was Justine Sternman and the letter I intended to deliver. There was no telling what response she'd have to learning about her true lineage.

And I wasn't forgetting Hilton Zeal, who had made an honest-to-goodness profession out of being a gangster.

*   *   *

As I said, the past week had been given to preparation for the upcoming trials. A day or so after the kidnapping, I sent Hush to release Sal Peretti from his subbasement cell. He returned the collection money and sent Sal on his way. That meant, even if Hush didn't say a word, Sal would stay out of my way.

Just after my meeting with Bernard Shefly, I called a man named Jacob Indigo.

"Hello," he said before the first ring was reported on my phone.

"Hey, Jake, it's Leonid."

"Mr. McGill."

"I need you to make me an introduction in the form of an invitation."

"Send me the dimensions, content, quantity, and any other particulars. I'll give you an estimate on the price in twenty-four."

I called another number later the same day. It connected me to an automated answering device that only beeped. I explained to the silent sentry of the telephone dimension all the ins and outs of the case so far.

*   *   *

EVERY DAY I WENT to Gordo's gym to shore up my aging physical prowess. This because when your father walks out, leaving you to fend for yourself, you learn certain lessons. One unalterable bit of knowledge is that in the end, it might come down to your life or the life of the man standing in front of you. Kill or be killed was on the menu for the next few days, so after Katrina and my father turned in, I took Twill to a twenty-four-hour diner six blocks from our Upper West Side domicile.

THE PINTA INN OVERINDULGED in a seafaring motif. There were real ships' wheels, replica anchors, framed lithographs of boats, and oil paintings of ships at sea.

Our waitress was Barbara Cutler, a Columbia journalism student who thought working in a diner would jump-start her investigative instincts.

"What can I get for you tonight?" Barbara asked us. She was a cross between American black and Irish Irish. Her face was broad, golden-hued, and freckled. Her light brown hair was kinky, fashioned into long braids.

"Just coffee, B," Twill said. "Can't be up to no good on a full stomach."

The waitress gave my son a winsome smile. She liked him; most women did. I'd've said he inherited his charm from my father if I didn't know they had nary a drop of blood in common.

After our coffees had been served, I asked Twill, "Are you ready?"

"Sittin' in a car, waitin' for a phone call . . . How hard could it be to get ready for that?"

"Getaway is an essential element of any job," I countered.

"Doesn't feel like it."

"What if you asked me to wait for you? What would you think if I didn't take it seriously?"

Twill heard. He shrugged and flashed a resigned grin.

"I need you to be armed, too," I said.

"Why?"

"Don't think of this as a one-off job. It's more like the first volley in a war. At any step along the way, we could find ourselves under attack."

"Then why we doin' it? We don't know Catfish or Lamont. They sure not payin' us enough to be puttin' this much on the line."

It wasn't a criticism. Twill really wanted to understand the inner workings of what I did.

"It was you singing," I said.

"Say what?"

"Yeah. You and Mardi singing. That's something I never

heard before. And like you said, Mardi is willing to help them. I mean...the first thing a parent learns about children is that you have to listen to them. You have to hear what they're telling you. Sometimes they might be talking about one thing but saying something else."

"So what did me and Mardi mean when we sang that little piece of a song?"

"Lamont was like Catfish's mouthpiece. Through him, Catfish was telling us how broken and misused him and his have been; how broken and misused all our people are." I hardly recognized myself in the words I was saying.

"I never heard you say *our people* before," Twill said, echoing my inner confusion.

When I was a criminal, most of Twill's life, I didn't have time for right and wrong. People were on the run, getting thrown on the scrap heap of prison, and hankering after revenge. Back then, there was no such word as *innocence* in my lexicon. An innocent man or woman was simply the lucky one found not guilty, or better, never even charged. I couldn't think of my victims other than as a means to an end. I was so hardened to suffering that somehow even the casualties of history fell outside the borders of my self-imposed sovereignty.

Catfish Worry's story and his immediate impact on me and mine had brought light to a lifelong blind eye turned toward my own grief. That sharecropper, that poor black man from Mississippi who dared to stand up to the oldest oppressors this nation had to offer, Catfish had given me drink and song and trust. These were sacred gifts and, in a way, I was born again.

"We better get to bed," I said. "Tomorrow's gonna be a long day."

I WAS SITTING IN the little front room waiting for the sun to rise when my cell phone rang. The caller was listed as UNKNOWN.

"Hello?" I said to the sneak who had gotten around all my protections.

"Somebody has put a hit out on you," a man's voice said. Then the call was disconnected.

That might have been the biggest surprise I had in the entire Catfish case. Captain Kittridge actually called and warned me. I didn't know if that was good luck or bad.

THE WEDDING WAS TO be an intimate affair at the Abbey of Christ's Redemption on a private estate in the Bronx. The property was so removed from the mainstream that not one out of a thousand New Yorkers would have known where to find it or, for that matter, that it even existed. I, as Lonnie Rudolf, had been selected to stand security outside the church, but that was cutting it too close for me to get the letter into Justine's hands before the ceremony. Even if I was technically successful, she might not have read it before saying *I do*.

Luckily the bride-to-be had decided to have a dinner for thirty-one of her closest girlfriends a few nights before the ritual. The restaurant was called Fancy Dan's, an establishment that specialized in haute cuisine and occupied the top floor of the China Citizens' Bank building near Park and Sixty-Fifth Street. The only problem was that Lonnie wasn't slated to work that event.

At 3:16 p.m. I was going through the office door of Alberghetti Security Services; they never used the acronym. The receptionist was a petite and lovely Asian woman in her early twenties. She sported turquoise tips and bright orange hair—heavily drenched in product. Her nameplate read LINDA.

Linda was chewing gum, studying her computer screen from under lashes not quite a foot long. I stood in front of her desk, waiting as she tapped long scarlet nails on the keys.

To my right, a sallow-skinned youth in a camel-colored suit sat on a sofa of similar hue. The camouflage made him at least partly blend with the upholstery. This young man was, of course, security for the security office. They didn't want to hide behind a locked door because that would make them seem weak. But they still needed to be safe. Therefore a living, breathing sentry had been provided.

I cleared my throat.

"Yeah?" said little Linda. She was none too pleased at being nudged.

"I'd like to speak to Antonio," I said as pleasantly as nature allowed.

If I haven't made it obvious before, I'm a brutal-looking man. Most women under the age of forty usually find me somewhere between off-putting and downright scary. It was the former with the fashion-plate secretary.

"You have an appointment?" she questioned. "Because if you don't, there's nothing I can do for you. We're very, very busy today."

"The Sternman thing, I know."

Linda stiffened while the camel camouflage sentry sat up a little straighter.

"Antonio is not seeing anybody," the young woman managed to say.

"Tell him it's Leonid McGill."

"You heard her, right?" Security inquired.

The young white man was still seated, but when I turned my head to regard him, he rose to the challenge. I didn't mind. After more than a week in the gym, I felt my testosterone levels running high.

"Mr. Alberghetti, we have trouble out here," Linda was saying.

At the same time, the slender youth in the bulky brown suit took a step in my direction. My age and height lulled him. The welcoming smile that crossed my lips came without a hint of what was about to happen.

"What's going on?" a pleasant tenor inquired.

That was Antonio. He didn't look like an Antonio. For that matter, he didn't much resemble my notion of somebody with the name Alberghetti. A man with a moniker like that should design men's suits or run an upscale Italian restaurant. He should have been tall and elegant, with silver-fox hair and manicured nails.

But this Antonio was five foot eight, with a bald head, bulging gut, and bowling balls for shoulders under a herringbone sports jacket.

Camel-flage took another step toward me.

"Hold it right there, Junior," Antonio said. "This man you're walking up on is Leonid McGill. He'll break half the bones in your body for business and the other half for fun."

Junior bridled a bit.

I dismissed him with a glance.

"Antonio," I said.

"Come on in before I have to find a new babysitter for Linda," the boss man replied.

ANTONIO HAD ONE OF those rare midtown offices that came with an outside deck. It was open-air and furnished with padded chairs, a small table, and a liquor cabinet.

"Whiskey?" my host offered after I was seated.

"Not right now." I wanted a drink. I wanted many drinks. But I had a job to do, and that task would brook no inebriety.

"What can I do for you, Leonid?"

"You can call me Lonnie to begin with."

"Lonnie?"

The name meant something to him, but he couldn't quite place it at first. Then the muscular security expert's eyes hardened like any creature coming upon a natural enemy in the wild.

I tried to look apologetic, but that didn't work.

"What the fuck are you trying to pull here?" he said.

"A simple delivery job," I replied. "I need Lonnie to work security for the party the bride-to-be is giving at Fancy Dan's. The entire process will be nonviolent, non-invasive, and in the end Justine Sternman would probably thank you. That is, if she ever knew you had anything to do with it."

"No," he said. "I will not compromise my principles, my livelihood, over some back-alley shit you're puttin' down."

I let the words and anger settle a bit. Then I nodded, trying to placate him. After all, he was bigger and stronger, and on top of that, he was well trained in the misnamed arts of self-defense.

"Whatever you say, Antonio. It's just that I hate to tell my client that I couldn't perform this simple, peaceful task because you slammed the door in his face."

"I don't give a fuck about you or whoever it was hired you," Alberghetti preached. "This is a goddamn honest business and I will not, will not be bullied, pushed, or intimidated."

When he quit the mob, Antonio went to college, "to learn how to talk bettah," he'd say to anyone who would listen.

He had succeeded—except when he lost his temper.

"You got some bourbon in the bar?" I asked.

"Fuck you and ya mothah."

"That an off brand?"

Antonio had a good sense of humor. He gave a two-syllable chortle, then went to the stand-up bar. Why not? He had the upper hand and the moral high ground too. He poured a ten-year-old, hundred-proof shot and a half of Barrell whiskey. It wasn't like the stuff Catfish paid me with, but I liked the taste. And I needed to cut the edge.

Antonio watched while I downed the whiskey.

"Anything else, Leonid?"

I took a deep breath and then stood looking out at the tall buildings that obscured the view of the East River.

"I guess not," I said. "Thanks for the drink. Gives me the strength for the next call."

"Okay," he said. "All right. I know you wanna tell me, so just spit it out. Who hired you?"

"Out-of-town gentleman name of Eckles."

Alberghetti gave me that natural-enemy look again, only this time it seemed more like he wanted to run than fight.

He looked around at the various corners of the patio; maybe Ernie had snuck in under my jacket.

"What's a Mississippi sodbuster got to do with a Daughter of the *Mayflower*?"

"That's his business, like this here is yours."

I did not enjoy threatening the self-made security man. He was a solid citizen who had done better than I at rehabilitating a life of crime.

Slowly, he lowered onto a chair, looking at me as if I was the bad news he'd been waiting for his entire life.

Behind his eyes, Antonio was trying to find the exit, the magic words to end the spell.

"So what is it you want?" he asked, the final capitulation.

I explained my need for Lonnie to be on guard near the diners.

"And what is it you plan to do?" he asked.

"I'll have a very official and sealed envelope with me. Inside will be a letter that the client wants young Miss Sternman to read. It's personal information with no threat of violence whatsoever. I'll pretend that someone hand delivered it down on the first floor."

"That's all?"

"That's it."

"What's the letter say?"

"Like I said, just some personal information. What she does with it is completely up to her."

"So there won't be any dead bodies found in the kitchen of Fancy Dan's?"

That was just Antonio trying to justify breaking an oath of protection. But it reminded me that, for all the bad men and bad intentions Catfish had stirred up, no one had actually died.

"If anybody gets killed," I said truthfully, "it will most probably be me."

"In that case," Alberghetti said on an up note, "go on. Knock yourself out."

I WENT TO MY office and changed into a black suit, white shirt, and blue tie. Before leaving, I placed two sheets of paper into a blood-colored leather briefcase. Then I took a taxi to the New Amsterdam Housing Project on West Twenty-Second. The man I'd come see lived on the eighteenth floor of the low-income apartment building. The monolith's elevators had been closed for repairs for at least seventeen months, so I had to rely on my feet.

There were two zigzag sections of eleven and then twelve stairs for each floor. The graffiti was entertaining, and there was hardly any smell at all.

"Hey, mistah," a young woman hailed when I was rounding the tenth floor. She was black-skinned with bright blond hair, half in braids. In her early twenties and built for trouble, she was swathed in a skintight maroon dress that wanted to find a party somewhere, anywhere.

She was the personification of an unwritten pop song, "Dead Man's Curves." But I appreciated the chance to stop and catch my breath. I had a penchant for trouble too.

"Hey, li'l sister," I said on a deep exhalation. "What can I do for you?"

"You got a cigarette?"

"If I did, I wouldn't be tryin' these damn stairs."

Her teeth were perfect, especially the left-side upper front; it was made from gold.

"That's a nice suit," she said. "You goin' to a party?"

"No. But if I was, I'd have a girl just like you on my arm," I said, thinking about the hormones my morning workouts churned up. "What's your name?"

"Esty."

"Never heard that name before." My breath was coming a little easier, but it was just as deep.

"Mama named me Ecstasy for its religious meanin'. But you men get so excited that I say Esty. And when they aks what it means, I tell 'em it got somethin' to do with Easter."

"You tellin' me what it means," I pointed out.

She shrugged and asked, "So where you goin'?"

"Up to see a man about a letter he got for me."

"Oh. Mr. Indigo."

"How could you tell that?"

"He a printah. Mama said he used to be a counterfeiter. They put him in jail, and aftah he got out, he just do invitations and like that." Esty had eyes that would follow you down into your dreams.

"Well," I said, "I better get back to it."

"What's your name?" she asked.

I told her and then continued my climb. She had nothing to do with Catfish's case, but I think of Esty from time to time. I remember her words and understand why young men put their lives on the line in everything from gangbanging to mountain climbing, from riding the roofs of subway cars to marching off to war.

"COME ON IN, MR. McGILL," Jacob Indigo said.

I didn't have time to ring. He was waiting just behind the door because we were both men who stuck to their schedules.

The entrance led into a large living room. It was hideously bright in there, but that had nothing to do with the sun. Indigo's windows were covered with thick black plastic sheeting affixed with electrical tape. The light came from six incandescent lamps designed to illuminate construction sites. The powerful twenty-four-hundred-watt lanterns stood on bright orange metal stalks like some kind of futuristic, robotic sunflowers.

All that wattage made the room stiflingly hot.

Along the wall of blacked-out windows stood a table at least eighteen feet long. It was high enough to work on while standing and was crowded with etching, printing, editing, and viewing devices.

"How you doin', Jake?"

Indigo was a smallish man with small palms that sported long fingers. His posture was slightly hunched over. He had tree-bark-brown skin with a lot of brick red folded in, and his gray-brown hair most resembled a heap of rags.

"Been thinking about getting a videocassette player," he said thoughtfully.

"VCR? Don't you know that they've graduated from DVD to thumbnail technology?"

"Yeah, yeah, yeah, yeah. I know. But I just bought twelve hundred twenty-nine videocassettes off'a Craigslist from a cat in Milwaukee. I want to start experimenting with false audiovisual images."

"Why don't you move to a nicer building first? I know you got the money."

Mr. Indigo stood up straight to answer that question.

"This was my mother's home," he said, his eyes entering a bad dream. "She cooked and cleaned, slept and had Bible meetings, right here in these rooms. While I was up at Attica, she died on this very floor. Asthma attack. Didn't find her for six days. If I wasn't such a fool, I might'a been here to save her life. . . ."

Signs of remorse are one of the intangibles they consider in the so-called justice system. It was no surprise that Jacob had been paroled sixteen months after his mother's death.

"You got what I need?" I asked, in part to distract him from the pain my previous question caused.

"The royal crest of Monaco was no problem. There was one on exhibit at a show at the Met last year. *Calling Cards of the Mighty—Crests, Seals, Devices, and Invitations.*"

He went over to the heroic table, donned a pair of latex gloves, and lifted a nine-by-twelve black envelope that was gilded around the edges. There was a pale-sapphire-colored label affixed to the face of the envelope. This was written upon in flourished script that read *Justine Penelope Sternman*. In the lower left corner of the back side, *PPN* was embossed in pink.

"You have the letter?" Indigo asked.

From my briefcase, I brought out the two sheets. One was the handwritten letter on the back of the ancient journal leaf. On top of that was an epistle I had penned.

Sad little Mr. Indigo inserted the pages. They fit perfectly into the counterfeit royal sleeve. Then he situated himself at the one clear spot on the table and went through the ritual of melting part of a wax stick on the fold at the back. After making enough of a hot-wax puddle, he applied a square black seal to make its false impression.

While going through this age-old process, he lectured:

"The envelope, handwriting, and dimensions were all

pretty simple. It's this wax that was the hardest thing to approximate. It had to be the right mix of red and lead white with just a hint of turpeth brown to make it creamy like raspberries."

He blew on the hot wax, appreciated his creation for a moment, then handed it to me.

I pretended to examine the workmanship, but I had no idea what it should look like. That's why I hired an expert.

"How much?" I asked while turning the royal missive from one side to the other.

"Twenty-three hundred sixty-two dollars rounded up from sixty-one thirty-five." Jake had that in common with Ernie Eckles—he knew to the penny what his work was worth.

THE ENTRANCE TO FANCY Dan's was at the north side of the China Citizens' Bank building. For once I eschewed the straightforward approach and went to the delivery entrance on the opposite side. There was a large truck parked in the loading dock and six or seven men unloading unwieldy office furniture from its trailer.

I walked right up to the guy who was overseeing rather than undertaking the heavy lifting.

"You in charge?" I asked the smallish supervisor. He

was in his forties and dark-skinned, most likely from somewhere on the subcontinent of India.

"Who are you?" he asked with no accent or sympathy.

"McGill," I said, my PI ID in hand. While he studied the card, I kept talking. "They got that Sternman event at Dan's tonight. My boss wanted me to go over any possible entrance other than the front door."

"Building supervisor already gave them the tour," the man said, shoving the identity card back at me.

"They asked me to double-check," I said patiently. "You know how it is."

You know how it is is a phrase that calls for its own interpretation. The little-big boss knew that giving me trouble would cause turmoil among the petty fiefdoms of the skyscraper. Private security would complain to Fancy Dan. Fancy Dan would call whatever party planner worked for the Sternmans, and then the supervisor would come back down and take away any overtime scheduled for the next month.

"McGill?" the petty overseer asked as if the name might have been pronounced *aardvark*.

"The only thing my people need to know is if there's a way to get to the special elevator entrance for the restaurant," I said.

"Nobody asked that," the supervisor admitted.

"What's your name?"

"Kal."

"Well, Kal, the people who run things above me are citizens. They look for vulnerability, whereas a man like me looks for opportunity."

The little man didn't know what to say to that, so he gestured me forward, and I was well on my way.

JUST BEYOND THE LOADING dock was a medium-size one-car lift that was used to deliver food and the like directly to the restaurant. On the other side of the service elevator was a well of stairs that brought me to the first-floor special entrance for the restaurant elevator.

Using this entry, I came up behind them.

Clarice Boorland sat behind a specially set-up desk blocking the express elevator. She was there to vet guests for the private party. Flanking Clarice were two well-built men, both of whom wore suits like mine.

"Hey, guys," I said.

The men turned first. They were broad-chested and wore blue ties, also like mine. Black suit, blue tie—that was the pedestrian uniform of Alberghetti's security team.

The woman stood and turned.

"Mr. Rudolf," she greeted, her voice heavy with sarcasm.

In her forties, Clarice was about five nine and had heavily processed black hair the luster of Royal Crown Russian sable. She was said to be preternaturally strong. One story had it that once a purse snatcher grabbed her handbag on Montague Street in Brooklyn Heights and ran. She went after him for seventeen or thirty-seven blocks, depending on who tells you the story. But whatever the details, when she finally cornered him, Willie Corbett turned, intending to slap the foolish woman down and make good his escape. All versions of the story, including Willie's, say that she hit him with a single right hook that put him down for the count.

"Ms. Boorland," I said, returning her derision with a boxer's respect.

"The boss says that you're working the entrance to the dining room tonight."

"The boss is always right," I said with a not-quite-winning grin.

Clarice knew that it would take more than a single blow to fell me.

Looking into my eyes, she called out, "Willie!"

From a different door on the far side of the elevator doors came a fleet-looking brown man. He also wore an ensemble like mine.

"Yeah, Clarice?"

"Mr. Rudolf here will be at the door upstairs. Why don't you go up there with him?"

"Okay." Willie Corbett, the man Clarice ran down and knocked out, was now her subordinate and live-in boyfriend—what some might call half a love story. She said that she'd never marry a purse snatcher but would keep him around until the real thing came along.

"WHAT THE HELL YOU doin' here, McGill?" Willie asked me when we were well on our way to the eighty-third floor.

"Same thing you're doing in Clarice's bed," I said. "Makin' a livin'."

Willie didn't like me, but that was okay. In my experience, there wasn't much profit from the appreciation of scavengers.

THE UPPER ENTRANCE TO Fancy Dan's main dining room comprised two great glass doors set at the end of a long hallway. The walls of that corridor were lined by shelving containing hundreds of horizontal bottles of wine.

My job was to stand to the side of the open doors and to be as innocuous as possible. Not a bad living for a man like Lonnie, a man with a high-school equivalency diploma and the willingness to stand in the path of physical threat.

The young women guests began to appear at around 8:00. They wore bright-colored gowns, many with short hems and décolletages. Of the thirty-one guests, two were Asian, one café-au-lait brown, and there were no Latinx guests at all.

BY 9:00 THE PARTY was in full swing. The volume rose while they made speeches, gave presents, drank deeply from the hallway of wines, and laughed and laughed and laughed. There were shrieks and shouts and incomprehensible declarations. I remember thinking that the only painter appropriate for this bacchanal would be a modern-day reincarnation of Hieronymus Bosch.

Willie Corbett had concealed himself around a corner somewhere. There to keep an eye on me while I stood guard over the young women's revel.

I was in no hurry.

At 10:47 a flagging damsel emerged from the contemporary saturnalia. She was tottering slightly and bound in a gown fabricated from the skin of some very young animal. She was blond that night, thin but well proportioned, and so used to high heels that she might teeter but never would she fall.

The heels had her at five seven. She smiled and held out a hand for me to take—for stability's sake.

"Excuse me," she said. "But is there another more private bathroom? I'm feeling a little sick."

"I bet we can find one," I assured her.

We went down the hall of wine and then toward a door in the outer chamber that had the word PRIVATE stenciled on it.

"Sounds like a bathroom could be in there," I said.

The young woman gave me a rather nauseated smile.

Six paces down and then to the right was a door upon which was affixed a red-and-white plastic sign that announced WOMEN.

"Here you go," I said.

"Will you come in with me?" she asked, obviously not put off by my brutish face and physique.

YOU CAN REALLY TELL poise and sophistication when a woman is on her knees, vomiting into a porcelain commode, and still manages not to get one spot on her unborn-lambskin gown. When she was done, I drenched my handkerchief in cold water and held it to her forehead.

"Oh my God, that feels good," she proclaimed. "Is this all part of what the security service has to offer these days?"

"No. It's steering three kids through childhood ill-nesses," I said. "Sometimes all on the same night."

"Children? You aren't wearing a ring."

"It's a compliment that you noticed."

"My name is Estelle Triumph."

"Leonid McGill."

"Do you have a card, Mr. McGill?"

ESTELLE DIDN'T NEED MY assistance on the walk back to her seat. But I accompanied her anyway.

Before sitting down, she whispered in my ear, "I use security sometimes. I'm going to call you." Then she lowered into her chair, and in a moment she was lost to me, like a fish darting off through the water after flopping out of the fisherman's boat. As I backed away from her, she was once again laughing, making exaggerated gestures, and listening without hearing a word.

Protocol would have me return to my post, but instead I moved toward the head of the table. The maître d'hôtel eyed me from the sidelines but decided not to interfere. After all, the rich women were only there to pad his pockets, not to open some new wound.

Justine was happy and laughing like the rest of the women. There was a small table placed behind her. This was heaped with unopened gifts. She, it seemed, wanted for nothing.

The first thing I noticed was her engagement ring: a diamond-crusted platinum band with a rectangular-cut deep-green emerald that was at least twenty karats in weight. It was a garish display. Everything else about the woman was understated and elegant. I had to wonder at the taste of the man she was marrying.

"Ms. Sternman," I said.

She didn't seem to hear, so I repeated her name.

"Yes?" Her tone was condescending, but I didn't hold that against her. It was quite a drop from her world into mine. I mean, she was the closest thing to royalty that America had to offer, and I was just a brown rowdy from down in the street somewhere.

"A man brought this downstairs. He claimed that he was representing the royal family of Monaco, but they wouldn't let him up." I handed her the forged envelope.

She took it from me and studied the two-thousand-dollar wrapper. I suppose that it passed muster, because she used her greasy steak knife to cut open the fold, and took the sheets out. She read the letter I had written first. It took about ninety seconds. Then she stood from the table like, I thought, Aphrodite rising from the sea. I had to catch the back of her chair to keep it from tipping over.

Justine was as tall as Estelle Triumph, but she wasn't wearing heels. Her cashmere dress was one-piece and teal colored, her lines perfectly proportioned. She was handsome with quiet dignity now that the party was behind her.

"Come with me." She turned and I followed.

A few of the revelers called to us, but Justine did not heed them. She went to the maître d'hôtel and asked him a question that I didn't overhear. He said something, then gestured toward a far corner of the dining room. She moved in that direction. I tagged along behind, wondering what she'd make of the words from her long-dead grandmother.

We came to a cream-colored door that had a digital lock on it. The maître d' must have given her the combination, because she pressed three buttons and pulled the door open.

It was a small room with four straight-backed wooden chairs around a square-shaped, solid wood table that had an empty ashtray at its center. There was a sink against one wall. The one window was floor to ceiling, looking down Park Avenue.

Justine sat at the table and took up the pages. I turned to face the window, giving her the illusion that she was not being watched. It was a simple ploy. The bright lights of the room cast her reflection perfectly in the glass.

She reread the letter I wrote and then held up the ancient sheet, supposedly torn from a journal that began on the *Mayflower*. She seemed to have the same trouble I did deciphering the ancient text. She put it down after a bout of squinting, holding the document at arm's length, and then bringing it to within an inch of her nose.

I thought she'd flip to the seventy-year-old letter on the back, but instead she picked up my note again.

I recalled the words as she reread them.

To Justine Penelope Sternman,

My name is unimportant. What is of interest is the letter written on the back of a page torn from the journal penned by one of your long-ago ancestors. My only job is to make sure you get this information. If, after reading the contents, you decide you want to meet the man in question, call the number at the bottom of the page. You will be connected to an answering service. Just give a time and place, and the party will meet you there. I apologize for the elaborate steps involved, but the phone must stay off because your father has threatened my quite elderly client. I need to make sure that he isn't put into jeopardy.

I cannot stress enough that there is no expectation on my part or on the part of the man who caused this information to be brought to you. If you want to burn the letter and forget it—that is your prerogative.
Thank you.

Miss Sternman then turned her attention to the back side of the journal entry. The letter Lucinda wrote was rendered in bright blue ink, and her granddaughter read it again and again. Now and then she looked at the other writings, but her main emphasis was on the intelligence her grandmother knew she needed.

There was a moment when she put the letter down, pondered two minutes or more, then took off her opulent engagement ring and dropped it into the envelope I had delivered. After that, she read the letter again . . . and again.

"Did you see who brought this?" she asked my back.

I turned to look at her. "No, ma'am."

"They told you it was a man?"

"I think so. Yeah, yeah. A guy said he had a message from some royals."

"A black man?"

"I don't know. Doesn't seem likely but . . ." I hunched my shoulders.

"What's your name?"

"Rudolf, ma'am. Lonnie Rudolf."

She bit her lower lip, looked out the window, and considered. She stood up, took in and then exhaled a deep breath.

"Mr. Rudolf, will you please go downstairs and ask the person who received this envelope to come up here?"

"Yes, ma'am."

I took two steps toward the door and then stopped.

"Excuse me, Miss Sternman."

"Yes, Mr. Rudolf?"

"Are you okay? I mean . . . is there anything else I can do for you?"

"No. I don't believe there is."

BACK ON THE FIRST floor, I told Clarice the story she should adhere to. Nothing I said made her happy. I needed her to tell Miss Sternman that indeed an envelope was delivered but the man who took it had gone off duty.

"Tell her that after the rush, you usually let a couple of guys go home," I suggested.

"I do not work for you, Leonid McGill," she told me. "And I'm not about to get knee-deep in your shit."

"I know you're not beholden to me, Clarice. But before you get all righteous and truthful with your betters, I suggest you call Antonio and ask him what he thinks."

*　　*　　*

THREE MINUTES LATER FOUND me crossing Park Avenue. It was just past 11:30, and the job I'd agreed to do was done. In many cases the next step was getting paid monies the client still owed. I would also, as a rule of thumb, be careful because of my proximity to the scene of my recent subterfuge. But the only thought on my mind was Justine Sternman putting her engagement ring in the sheath with her grandmother's letter. What was the heiress thinking? I felt as if my life and hers were being guided by the dead hand of the past, as Marx taught me through my father's homeschooling before Dad left us to struggle and my mother to die.

This reverie was broken by a triple honk on a car horn. Even before I could look up, there came the screech of tires. I heaved to the left, hitting the grass of the avenue divider with my shoulder. The pistol was in my hand; two men were coming up from behind me; they were also armed. But before any shots could be fired, a yellow cab bounced up on the median and headed straight for my shadows.

One guy jumped out from in front of the headlights, but the cab broke hard and swung to the right, hitting the gymnast gunsel with the passenger's-side door. The other attacker was even more acrobatic. He leaped up on the hood and then belly flopped on the car's roof. In response, the cab accelerated and then hit the brakes again. The second man was thrown hard to the pavement.

By then I was on my feet, and the taxi pulled up almost as if I were an everyday fare. I pulled open the back door, jumped in, and the taxi took off.

Twill guided the car into the street, among blaring horns and shrieking brakes. Then he ran a red light and swiveled into an illegal turn down a comparatively quiet crosstown street.

We were headed west.

"Damn, Pops," my daredevil son exclaimed.

"I guess one of the guys I talked to must have let Hilton know. Probably Shefly."

"Why didn't they stop you coming in?"

"I used an alternate entrance."

I stayed flat in the back seat, not due to fright but rather because my mind was so fixed on the problems at hand that my physical position seemed...inconsequential.

"You okay?" Twill asked.

"Bring us to the Eighty-Sixth Street parking garage."

"Truth to that."

*   *   *

A FEW MINUTES AFTER midnight, in the little front room of our vast four-bedroom prewar apartment, Twill and I unpacked the events of the evening. My wife and father were asleep in their beds. My other children, Shelly and Dimitri, didn't live at home anymore. Shelly was in a dormitory at college, and D lived with a Belarusian femme fatale, who, as my wife said, would either kill him or make him into a man—or both.

"You think they were gonna kill you?" my son asked.

"I don't know. Zeal does play for keeps, and those guys were good. Thank you, boy."

"She get the letters?" he asked.

"Got 'em, read 'em, and removed her engagement ring."

"So what do we do now? Hit the mattresses?"

I'd made sure that all my children were schooled in the classics of Hollywood and European film history. They knew *Casablanca, The Third Man, The Seventh Seal,* and Gary Cooper's *Virginian,* circa 1929. *The Godfather* was definitely on their syllabus.

"No," I said. "First I need to go to the Port Authority bus station to meet a guy at 5:47. While I'm doing that, you tell your mom and grandfather that Hush will be by to take you all someplace safe."

"You don't need me with you?"

"I can't have my son save my ass more than once in a two-week period. That happens and my forced-retirement clause automatically kicks in."

TWILL WENT OFF TO bed, and I napped on the little den's sofa for a few hours. I didn't want to climb in bed with Katrina for fear that she might wake up and ask me to explain why I was putting our son's life on the line with my own. There was really no way for me to explain how keeping Twill close to me, even in dangerous situations, was better than leaving the young man to shift for himself. The spirit of the law was Twill's heart, but he had no truck with lawmakers or their enforcers. He knew that a poor woman wasn't going to get a fair trial; that the laws were made for the rich to pick the pockets of everyone else; and that, at the crux of it, the only real law was the one that nature provides.

My job was to steer him along until his survival instincts matched his natural intelligence.

I WAS FLOATING JUST below the surface of consciousness when my phone clicked. If I'd been a caveman, it would have been the broken twig before the greatest war in unrecorded history.

I picked up the cell, turned it on in the dark, and saw the text.

Not safe at the place I said. ma

I got the message, closed my eyes, and fell into a deep sleep as secure as a baby, safe in the womb of life.

THE 5:47 FROM MEMPHIS was due in at Gate 14. I sat across the aisle in the waiting area for Gate 15, where the bus from Buffalo was due at 6:59. Pretty much alone in that area, I sat with my back to the Memphis gate. It was only on days like these that I wore my olive trench coat and gray fedora. The hat helped to conceal my identity, while the back collar of the coat hid a microlens developed by Bug Bateman. The lens's Bluetooth connection to my cell phone gave me a good view of the Memphis gate and those waiting there.

In my opinion, there were two possibilities. One was a skinny forty-something white guy dressed in faded jeans, a well-worn blue T-shirt, and a Cardinals baseball cap. He was traveling with a drab green duffel and carried a brown paper bag that could have held a half-pint of whiskey, a small lunch, or a weapon. Four seats away and across the row from him sat a hale black man sporting an overabundance of coifed facial hair, almost a mask. This healthy specimen, who could have been in his thirties, wore a loud red ensemble you'd expect on the hipster interpretation of urban Santa Claus.

THERE WERE EIGHTEEN OR so others. Some waiting to board the Memphis bus back down south and others who were meeting loved ones. These bystanders were white and black and brown, young and old, men and women.

The citizens waiting were, on the whole, solitary units. The few who clung together broke down on color lines. One exception to this rule was a black woman somewhere in her forties and a thirty-something white woman. They spoke to each other, crossing their arms in that familiar and yet distant way that strangers do when they decide to speak. The black woman wore a lovely blue-and-silver dress with the fur and hide of some kind of vermin draped across her shoulders. What really got me was her blue hat. The brim was large and malleable. She'd worked it so that the shade dipped down over her left eye and behind her head while the other side rose over her right eye, almost like an introduction. I love black American women in hats. It reminds me of church, even though I am an atheist, and also of the nobility that mobs of men like me are destined to slaughter.

The white woman had a bright pink carry-on suitcase with four wheels. She wore a one-piece polyester dress that was patterned with bright yellow and deep brown squares. She had a long, equine face and big eyes that wandered aimlessly, looking at nothing.

"You probably think it's the brothah in red," a disturbingly familiar voice said from my right.

I didn't turn. There was no reason to.

"The guy in the baseball cap is a likely candidate," I suggested.

"Uh-uh, main. White guy stand out in a crowd like that there. People, both black and white, remembah him."

"So we move on the one in red?"

"Why? It ain't him."

"No?"

"It's the one with the pink suitcase. The girl."

I oriented the phone screen on the polyester white woman. She was a few inches taller than I and in better shape than you would guess at first glance.

"I see," I said. "You know the woman she's talking to."

"That's it, McGill. Alberta Jackson. She were married to my half brother—Israel."

"If she's family, what's she doing here?"

"Her and Izzy didn't break up too well."

The pathos inside those last words caused me to turn and regard my pickup partner. Ernie Eckles looked exactly the same as he did when we first met. He was the kind of farmer who went to the country store once a year and bought three pairs of pants and shirts of the same cut and color.

"What you plan to do about her?" I asked the killer.

"Nuthin'. I mean, I might wanna kill her, but she's my two favorite nephews' mother. And she went through hell with Israel."

"Door's opening," I said. "Bus must be here."

Ernie's ex-half-sister-in-law moved quickly to get behind her white friend as Polyester Girl rolled her pink bag to the far left side of the door. It was a good move, though not good enough to fool an old pro like Ernie. And yet something about the way she positioned herself made me believe that she had a better plan.

Ernie had the same idea.

"You right," he told me. "Prob'ly baseball cap."

"Could be both," I opined. "You know, in twenty-first-century New York, white and black have learned to work together."

"Maybe so."

"If I were to go against you again, I'd prefer three lines of fire."

"That'd do it."

"You agree?" I asked.

"Yep. Redbeard and Red Cap, too."

The men he spoke of positioned themselves at equidistant positions, forming a semicircle around the door. The black man had his left hand in a red pocket. The white guy held the paper bag close to his chest.

"Somebody paid a fuck of a lot of money to see me dead," Ernie muttered.

"Your friend Catfish made a threat that goes all the way down to the first nerve of America."

"We bettah move on before the bus empty out. They might start lookin' round when I don't show."

We walked away from the waiting area just as the first passenger emerged from the gate door. The killing crew wasn't looking anywhere but there.

THERE'S A BREAKFAST PLACE on Thirty-Third Street near Eighth Avenue. It doesn't have a name, but the cook is French and the omelets are too.

"Damn," Ernie said. "This some good shit here."

I sipped my coffee and took a bite of sage-accented sausage.

"I plan to retire next year," he said. "At least I will if I live that long."

"You're not even fifty, are you?"

"This ain't a old man's trade."

"Now you tell me."

Then for a while we ate in silence.

After some minutes, he said, "I got Alberta's address around somewhere."

"I thought you said you were going to leave her alone."

"I said I'm not gonna kill her. But she might know somethin' give us a little edge."

"I already got a good idea," I said.

"I needs facts, not ideas."

LATER THAT MORNING FOUND us at the corner of Second Avenue, one block up from Ninety-First.

"Why don't we just go up and ring the bell?" I asked.

"Because it's Wednesday," Ernie said with certainty.

"Wednesday?"

"Alberta always goes to confession on Wednesday mornings. She was gonna slaughter me, so then, after maybe an hour of lookin', she had to go explain why her information about me bein' on that bus was wrong. They'll scare her a little bit, and then you better believe she's gonna run for the safety of the church. I figure she'll be back here in somewhere around twenty minutes or so."

I didn't argue, because we were out of my depth. Maybe Ernie was right about Alberta. Even if he wasn't, we were standing less than a block away from her apartment building. Sooner or later, something was bound to happen.

"How did you know that they'd be waiting for you?" I asked.

"The ticket taker at the bus depot in Clarksdale is Mattine Hogarth, cousin to Myrtle Jennings. Myrtle is from around where I come from, and she's friends with Alberta. When I bought my bus ticket, Mattine got all nervous, like she didn't know whether to smile or cry, know what I mean?

"I figured somethin' was up. Anyway, half the time I abandon my ticket and take a detour."

"Everybody's gotta change sometime," I said. Ernie smirked and nodded.

"You say Catfish is all right?" the killer asked.

"As well as a man in his nineties can be after gettin' shot in the shoulder."

"An' you shot the guy got him?"

"My son did," I said. "I wasn't there. But the shooter is gonna live too. I saw him just after the shootout."

"Look," Ernie said, gesturing with his chin.

Miss Jackson's floppy blue hat jounced on the way up

to the front door of a brick apartment building. She ministered over the lock and then went in.

Ernie stared after her for a while, then said, "Let's go."

I picked the front door lock just to show Ernie I could.

Alberta lived on the ninth floor of the well-appointed residence. Ernie and I took the stairs and then waited behind the door that opened onto her floor. Somewhat surprising to me, Ernie took out a cell phone and entered a number.

"Myrtle?" he said after the span of three or four rings. "Yeah, baby, it's me. Yeah, yeah. I'm up here in New York, and I thought I might get together with Bert. You know there's been too much bad blood, and I wanna see if she'll accept my apologies. She still live at that place on Second Avenue between Ninety-One and Ninety-Two, right?...Uh-uh, no, no, honey, you don't have to call her. I'm just gonna drop by.... Yeah, like family."

He disconnected the call, pushed open the door to the hallway, and led the way till we were standing on either side of number 914. We'd been waiting four minutes when the lovely rose-brown woman came out toting a diminutive brown suitcase in each hand. I was on the side leading toward the small elevator, so Alberta turned toward me. She'd changed into sleek brown slacks and a billowy, silken blue T with yellow flowers of some kind stenciled here and there.

We stood eye to eye. I smiled and gave a small nod. She did an about-face, coming nose to Adam's apple with the Mississippi Assassin.

"Hey, Bert," he said, smiling broadly.

"Oh no," was her reply.

"Can we come in?"

I LIKED EVERYTHING ABOUT Alberta Jackson. Her styled short hair, her bright skin that was an equal mixture of copper and gold, the comfortable furniture in her living room, and the framed photographs of her and her sons, when they were all ten years younger, hanging on the wall. I liked everything about Alberta Jackson, and so her fear and consternation ate at me.

She sat at the edge of a stuffed chair upholstered in reds and violet. I was perched on a matching piece two yards away. Ernie remained standing, his back against a yellow wall.

"You, you want me to g-get you sumpin' to drink, drink, Ern?"

"I'm not here to hurt you, girl," he replied.

I'm sure that Ernie's promise was meant to put her at ease, but instead it seemed to harden her resolve. Her eyes tightened and her lips wanted to curl into a sneer.

"You not?" she spat. "You don't think it hurt a woman

to be burned outta her home? You don't think it hurt to be driven outta town an' tore away from her chirren?"

Ernie's usually emotionless face was suddenly etched with feeling.

"You know I didn't have to do with any'a that," he said.

"Maybe not by hand, but it's cause'a you that nobody would help me. It's cause'a you that my sons are growin' up without a mother's love."

"You stepped out on Israel, baby."

"An' how many times you think that no-good half brother'a yours done done me dirt in the street?"

That accusation actually made Ernie look away.

I sympathized with the woman. Judging by his expression, Ernie did too.

There was anger, remorse, and even self-recrimination dancing between the killer's eyes and lips, cheeks and brow.

"I'll make you a deal," he said after a few scowls. "You tell me everything about how you got to that bus station this morning, and I will get you back home with Karnak and Troy."

Their eyes met with such intensity that I began to feel intangible.

Ernie's aspect turned stoic again. He had offered a solution and so was no longer compelled to feel guilt. Alberta, on the other hand, needed to climb over the jagged terrain of pain, fear, and distrust to get to a place where she could even consider entertaining an armistice. Her inner rage was so hot that she shook. I'm pretty sure that she wanted to scream.

It took a few minutes for all that to pass.

"A man come to me," she began. "He the one want you dead."

"What man?" I asked, in an attempt to remain solid.

"White man."

"There's a whole lotta white men in New York," I countered.

"He'idn't gimme no name. Forty-sumpin', prob'ly. Brown hair and his left arm was in a sling."

"What this one-armed white man say?" Ernie asked.

"He wanted to know how to find you if you come to New York. I told him that you was like a ghost, that you never rested your head on the same pillah twice. I told him that that was for the good, 'cause he'd be bettah not findin' you. I said that lookin' for you was like lookin' for Spanish flu."

"An' what he say?"

"He was all smug. Said he had fifteen thousand dollars for the man or woman could put a finger on you—more if that man or woman helped set you up."

"Why'd he even think I'd be comin' up here?" Ernie asked.

Not minding the question, I feared the answer.

"He said that a man told him that you hired a detective or sumpin'."

Ernie looked at me.

I shrugged.

"And you asked Mattine to tell Myrtle when I got on that bus," Ernie said to his favorite nephews' mother.

Alberta didn't answer that question.

"You don't have to worry 'bout your friends," he said. "Me bein' sloppy ain't their problem."

That softened Bert a bit.

"I get how the pieces fit," Ernie continued. "But the thing I don't understand is how the white man in the sling knew to come to you in the first place."

"Montgomery."

"Monty Morrison? That boy done lost his mind?"

"He deep into the opioids. All they have to do is give him some pocket change, an' he'd send his own mama to hell."

"How'd they know to go to this Monty?" I asked, still trying to maintain substance in that hyperreality.

"That niggah brag about anything," she told me. "You bettah believe he done said to a dozen peoples that he knew the Mississippi Assassin."

"So you went down to the bus station with that white woman and her friends to point me out and collect your blood money," Ernie stated. It wasn't actually an accusation, but considering the source—it was serious speculation.

A tremor ran along Alberta's neck, but she didn't fold.

"They gimme the money up front and promised ten more if you died."

"How about the bus station's video cameras?" I asked. Professional curiosity.

"They said somebody was gonna turn 'em off."

"What if I didn't die?" Ernie asked.

Alberta looked at her ex-half-brother-in-law with an eye as cold and clear as the polar sun.

"If they killed you," she said, "I could go home and take Israel to court ovah my sons. If they only wounded you, I figured I'd have enough time and money to take Troy and Karnak outta Mississippi. Now that I had the money for that."

Ernie was looking down at the floor. I believed that I knew what he was feeling, that all these years he'd thought he was doing one thing, but really all he was was wrong.

He raised his head to regard Alberta. She swayed back an inch or two.

After a long moment, he said, "Keep them bags packed, Bert. After I clear this mess up, I will bring you home."

ON THE STREET IN front of Alberta's apartment building, Ernie told me that he had a few things to take care of. We made plans for a later rendezvous and went our separate ways.

I HADN'T BEEN ALONE in my office in quite a while. I actually missed Mardi and naturally worried about Twill. But if life has taught me anything, it's that you had to survive desertions, abandonments, and loss—no matter the cause.

I took a burner phone from my pencil drawer and fired it up.

There was one message.

"This is Justine Sternman," her recorded voice declared. "The contents of my grandmother's letter came as no surprise. Nine years ago I took a DNA test with some friends at college. It was an anonymous test, as I am a Sternman and our bloodline is considered more valuable than any other possession. You must know what I discovered in that report. I took three other blind tests, and they all turned out more or less the same...."

Something about her tone made me trust that she was telling the truth. Trust is the most dangerous emotion for a man in my business.

"...that said, I would very much like to meet with you, him, my grandfather. I know you said that I could choose the place, but if my father is suspicious, I cannot presume that he won't be monitoring me. So I ask that you send an email addressed to Lolo at banabana @PQR1.nono, giving the place and time of your choosing. And tell my grandfather that I look forward to meeting him."

I figured that the email address was connected to one of her computer-nerd friends. It was probably safe, but I forwarded the information and address to my own private nerd—Bug Bateman. He'd send the message and monitor its progress. The time and place were to be Bellingham's English Eaterie at 7:30 that evening.

IN THE LATE AFTERNOON, at an upscale hamburger stand in the basement of Grand Central Station, Ernie and I approached a man sitting at a small round table in a corner. Hush's back was against the wall. In front of him was a milkshake and a triple-decker cheeseburger in a red plastic basket.

Hush stood and extended a hand. Ernie accepted the

offer. They held each other's eye for two seconds, maybe a little less. Then we all sat.

To anyone around, we looked like three men who probably worked together, stopping for a bite at the end of a long day. That observation would be mostly true, the only difference being that our work hadn't yet begun.

"Nice to meet ya," Ernie said. "I been hearin' 'bout you for years."

"Me too," Hush replied. "I even caught a glimpse of you one time."

"Oh? Where was that?"

"In Vegas eight years ago. You were coming out of Tony Violet's office at that casino he ran."

"Tony died the night I met him."

"So did Arnold Gorham," Hush said. "Him and Tony really hated each other."

"Can I get you something to eat, Ernie?" I asked.

"I don't eat meat."

"Not even fish?"

"Fish flesh is still meat. Don't worry about me."

Standing in line, I had time to think about the depths of the investigation, such as it was. Usually a PI, even one with a criminal history like mine, spends his (or her) exertions in shadows unknown and unsuspected by the people he's up against. Most of the time, my targets never knew I'd even been there. And on those rare occasions when I have been revealed, I was still the most dangerous man in the room.

"What can I get for you, sir?" a middle-aged white woman asked me. She had pink hair and three visible, if fading, tattoos.

"Triple cheese, garlic fries, and three beers, please."

"I have to take the caps off the beers," she apologized. "They can't leave the dining area."

I nodded. She tapped around on the register and came up with a price, which I paid. She handed me a small plastic disk along with the change.

"It'll light up and vibrate when your order is ready," she advised.

STANDING NEAR THE PICKUP station, I looked over the people in and outside the dining area. There were hundreds eating, milling around, or walking with purpose to or from a gated platform. No one looked like an immediate threat.

This reconnaissance was reflex on my part. Hush and Ernie would have seen any danger before I did. Hush and Ernie, professional killers kickin' it at a hamburger stand.

Again I wondered about the steps that brought me

to that juncture. It had to do with Twilliam and Mardi singing the blues alongside of Lamont. And Lamont himself so committed to his great-great-grandfather. There was Catfish jumping out of his blues waters into the killing boat of his son. I felt a kinship to all of them, more biology than psychology, more mortal than divine.

The disk came alive with seven winking red lights, and then it began to pulsate. The timing made me laugh.

HUSH AND ERNIE WERE still sitting at the little table, comfortable and quiet. If anyone bothered to really pay attention to them, they might have realized that their own pathetic lives were being played out like late-night reruns on a second-rate cable station.

"You got any kids, Ernie?" I asked just before taking a bite out of my triple cheeseburger.

The question threw him. His brows knit, but then he smiled.

"Six," he said with pride. "An' they all beautiful."

Hush nodded, then looked at me. "You think we can get outta this mess without any heavy lifting?"

"I really don't know. I mean, if I were in their position, I'd think twice before poking the gorilla. And the damage was already done, years ago."

"What you mean by that?" Ernie asked.

I told them about Justine's blood tests.

"How bad is this Hilton dude?" Ernie asked.

"He thinks he's untouchable," I said.

Ernie smiled. "What about Justine? What you think she's up to?"

"She says she wants to meet with Catfish."

"When?" That was Hush.

"Tonight."

"At my place?"

"Catfish with you?" Ernie chimed.

"Yeah. Place I got north of the city. Always room for one more."

I said, "Tell Twill to get to Bento's with Mr. Worry by seven forty-five."

"Who's Twill?" Ernie asked.

"The new generation," Hush replied.

I GOT TO BELLINGHAM'S Eaterie at 7:47. The place was filled with people off from work at their Wall Street grinds. It was a very large room, the center of which was occupied by a circular bar manned by six bartenders attempting valiantly to meet the orders of the many dozens of patrons and waitpersons. The rest of the room was temporarily colonized by two hundred or more diners. The pedestrian volume of the dining room was as loud as Grand Central at rush hour—and then there was the soundtrack: music from the sixties to the eighties pumped up to the max.

Jerome Eastwood was standing at the host's podium, a stately gentleman who learned his manners before his ABCs. He spoke with a genteel English accent even though he'd been born in Omaha half a century before.

Jerry and I had a strictly pecuniary relationship. I'd make a reservation at the restaurant for a Mr. A. K. Fox. After making the reservation, I'd send an email with instructions about what I needed from him. For this service, I showed up and gave him three crisp one-hundred-dollar bills.

"Mr. Fox," Jerry greeted.

"Mr. Eastwood. The joint seems to be jumpin' tonight."

"That's because tomorrow they could well be leaping from a window if China presses back hard enough on these tariffs."

I nodded sagely and asked, "Is she here?"

"Having sparkling water at table nine."

"In fifteen minutes, have one of your staff tell her about the door beyond the ladies' room."

"As you say, Mr. Fox."

When we shook hands, I passed him the cash. After that, I sauntered off toward the bar.

I ordered a snifter of Hennessy Paradis from a bartender who had as a wedding ring the tattoo of a coiled green snake. She was an ash blonde with pale skin and blue eyes that glinted like electric sparks. When she brought my hundred-fifty-dollar drink, I smiled and said, "Not so easy to take off a wedding band like that."

"That's what he thinks." She smirked, and I toasted her cynicism.

Table nine was out of the line of sight from my position at the bar. That is, except for a mirror hanging from one of the posts holding up the shelving. Through that small window, I could see Justine Sternman in a conservative gray dress suit sipping effervescent water and looking around pensively. She was alone, and I couldn't make out anyone else watching her.

The cognac was very good. Not ecstatic like Eckles's bootleg, but what was?

A waitress clad in the prescribed LBD walked up to table nine. If I didn't know better, I would have thought the server was asking Justine did she need anything else? The waitress departed, and my target waited ninety seconds or so before getting up and heading for the toilet.

The waitress had told Justine to take a door beyond the entrance to the restroom. The door was usually locked, but it would be open when she tried it. There was a similar door beyond the men's room. I took that exit, following a long corridor behind the back wall of the restaurant until I came upon the ultrasocialite in the pearl-gray dress.

"Oh!" she said, tensing at the sight of me. "Mr. Rudolf? They ... the woman downstairs at the restaurant told me that you, you went off duty. And so did the man who received my letter. . . . I don't understand."

"I doubt that," I said. "You're a smart woman, Miss Sternman. My real name is McGill. Leonid McGill. You can appreciate that I've had to be careful. The men after your grandfather have already tried once to kill him."

"Kill him," she repeated the words.

"Someone feels strongly that his blood should not be recognized in your line."

"My father."

"How many cell phones do you have?"

"One. Why?"

I took a glistening bag from my sports-coat pocket, saying, "A man with enough money could have somebody trace your phone even without a bug. This bag will make sure that doesn't happen."

She handed me the phone; I sealed it in the bag and then put the bag in my pocket.

"How do you know that I don't have some other kind of tracking device on me?" she asked.

"I don't. That there is what is known as an article of faith."

"Faith in what?"

"In my assumption that you would not knowingly involve yourself in the murder of an innocent man."

"You can't be certain of that," she said.

"I can't be certain that I'll wake up tomorrow morning. That doesn't keep me from sleeping like a baby. Shall we go?"

"Go where?"

"I have your grandfather somewhere close."

Justine looked deeply into my eyes. I don't know what she was searching for, or if she found it. But she gestured with her left hand, and I led the way.

IN ALMOST EVERY WAY, Bento's was the opposite of Bellingham's. It was a sedate Japanese restaurant with tables up front and private dining rooms in back. A middle-aged Japanese woman dressed in what I can only assume was traditional garb took us to one of the back rooms. She pulled open a jade-green door and ushered us in.

Twill was there with Catfish Worry, the elder's arm no longer in a sling. Catfish stood and took two steps toward us as the door to our small room closed behind.

Young white hands and ancient brown fingers reached out for one another.

"Ain't you sumpin'?" the grandsire said.

"Mr. Worry."

"Everybody call me Catfish, girl."

"I've dreamt about you for years."

They were both near tears.

"I been seein' you since before you was born." Catfish whispered so as not to break the spell.

Twill got to his feet, putting a hand on the old man's shoulder.

"Hm?" Catfish glanced at my son, who nodded toward the table. "Oh yeah. Come on, child. Let's sit. You hungry?"

"No, Grandfather. No."

They sat side by side while Twill and I stood sentry at the door. I suppose we should have left the room, but there was something gravitational about the meeting between the *Mayflower* and the deep cleft of slavery that followed in its wake.

"Why didn't you and my grandmother stay in England?" Justine asked. The question was so gently put that there was no hint of accusation.

"I was already wed to a beautiful woman name of Ernestine Charles. We had four chirren down Mississippi an' I loved 'em all. An' Ernestine needed a man, the father of her boys and girls. I loved your grandmother too, but one day her father would'a fount out, he would. And then what would'a become'a Lu and our son?"

"My father," Justine allowed. "He tried to kill you."

"I shouldn't'a gone to 'im. I shouldn't'a made him scared like that. His whole life he's been a white man, and there I come kickin' that high ladder right out from under him."

"But he had no right to hurt you, no cause." The blueblood took the bluesman's hands again.

"You sayin' that 'cause you from a inside world, girl."

"What does that mean?"

"You cain't see the ugliness, the need in people who been broke down and walked on."

"Need? He needs to hate you?"

"I been playin' in juke joints from Selma to Yokohama for ovah seventy years. People love my blues 'cause it talk to 'em. It wash over 'em an' pulls out they pain. Charles must'a suspected that there was a secret like me off in the high grass somewhere. I'm just glad it turned out to hate rather than in on him."

This last declaration set Justine back in her chair.

"People like me play to that darkness," Catfish continued. "We put to song what make a grown man cry."

The hand on my shoulder made me aware that I was leaning toward the newfound blood relations.

"Let's go out, Pops," Twill said.

I ORDERED TWELVE PIECES of toro sashimi. Twill got a tempura fish plate.

When my gut was full of fatty tuna, I looked up at Twill and said, "My father left me when I was a boy."

"I know," he said.

"I never wanted that to happen to my kids."

"We're all with you, Dad. No matter what happens, we're with you."

MAYBE AN HOUR LATER, Catfish and Justine came out from their private confessional. They seemed pleased and relieved, pensive and, in Justine's case, determined.

"So?" I asked when they joined us at our table.

"Is my grandfather still in danger, Mr. McGill?"

"Black man in danger if he wake up early or sleep in late," Catfish answered.

I smiled. "Yeah. He's in danger."

"What can I do?"

"Set up a meeting with your father. Tomorrow afternoon at a place called Mama So's."

"Where's that?"

"Don't worry. His people know."

"I need an address. I want to be there too."

"Why did you take off your engagement ring after you read that letter?" I don't know why I asked.

"Because I knew that it was a symbol for my father and all the people faithful to him."

"You didn't know that before?"

"I did, but it was never in words. It was something I couldn't say, even to myself. But when I read Grandmother Lucinda's letter, I knew the life I was living was a lie. I was just keeping up appearances because no one knew the truth."

"Part of the lie was your wedding?"

"Yes."

"And you think the truth will be in that room with your father and Catfish?"

"Yes."

At almost any other time, I would have said that either I go alone or I drop the case. But there was something about seeing Catfish and Justine together that placed a limit on my sense of authority.

"Your father is in with some bad people, Justine. There's a man named Zeal, and a whole raft of killers come along with him."

"I understand you're trying to protect me, Mr. McGill.

Grandfather told me that you took his case for a bottle of whiskey. I'll pay your fees and expenses, but I have to be at that meeting."

"What do you say, Catfish?" I asked.

"Why are you asking him?" Justine said.

"Because he's my client, not you."

"Well," Catfish Worry began, "I know these some bad people. But this girl got her grandmother's heart. I don't want her there, but I think she got to be."

It was the wrong way to play it. I knew that. But this whole case was like the wisdom of a boxer: *If you don't want to get hit, you should stay out of the ring.*

"Twill."

"Yeah, Pops?"

"You're going to take Catfish and Justine up to Nyack tonight. Tomorrow at four, bring them to Mama's."

Twill gave me a quarter nod.

"I'll get the word to your old man's people when and where to meet," I said to Justine.

"Thank you, Mr. McGill," she said.

Her gratitude felt like the condemned offering her executioner a good-morning smile.

"Keep it," I said.

*　　*　　*

EVERYTHING WAS SET BY ten the next morning. Thugs and socialites, blood letters and bluesmen, were all ready to read their lines and make their vows.

I was sitting at Mardi's desk—the only beating heart in the office complex. Some days, when you're sitting alone with the truth, you question whether or not there'll be a tomorrow. That was one of those days for me.

When mortality weighs heavily like that, people are apt to make odd choices. I guided my internet provider to the *New York Times* website and read those articles they made available. I don't usually read the news. My experience has been that at its best, news reporting is an approximation of the slant on the truth that reporters, editors, and advertisers want the public to know.

But that day, I don't know why, I wanted to be entertained by trying to figure out the truth behind the half lies. I skipped ten or twelve stories about the president. Finance held no interest. I did come across one interesting item.

A few minutes past two on the previous afternoon, at a flophouse in Brownsville, an African American man known only as Monty was found dead on the roof. He'd been shot in the forehead and must have died immediately. There were no witnesses. No one heard the gunshot. There was no suspect, and even though Monty was a heroin addict, it wasn't clear why he was killed.

The phone rang. I knew the number on the display panel.

"Hello, Katrina. You know you shouldn't be using your cell when I got you with Hush."

"I don't like that man. He's cold inside."

"Believe me when I tell you that cold is the only way you want him."

"I need to talk to you about something," she said.

"Twill told you what was going on, didn't he?"

"Yes. You're trying to help that nice man Mr. Worry."

"So, knowing that, couldn't this wait till tomorrow?"

"I'm in love with your father," my wife of a quarter century said.

It was that good left hook you'd been trying to stay away from for nine rounds; the one chance your opponent had of putting you down. A knockout punch when victory was almost in reach.

I wasn't so much thinking about boxing as feeling it. My muscles tensed with shoulders hunched up high. If I wasn't seated at Mardi's desk, I would have probably gone to one knee.

While I grappled with these physical responses, Katrina kept talking. She said that nothing had happened, that my father had been a perfect gentleman. While they were out at Nyack, she had finally revealed her feelings to him. He told her that he would never cross that line — he would rather die.

In the ring of my mind, the referee had counted eight and I was up on my feet. I was hurt, but there was no pain. Instead there flowed the numbness that had been the solace of my childhood.

"Katrina," I said, cutting off her endless explanatory chatter.

"Yes, dear?"

"Why would you choose this moment to tell me this? Matter of fact, why tell me at all?"

I was dead inside; outside she was silent.

After a few moments of this standoff, I sighed.

"We'll talk when I see you tonight," she said.

"You ever think about what it's like to act in one of those long-running plays on Broadway?" I said.

"What?"

"One'a those plays," I repeated. "You know, by some playwright who used to be good but now his stuff is just okay but people go to see it anyway because he used to be good."

"I don't understand what you're saying, Lee."

"Imagine you have a middle-size role in a play like that," I went on. "Like maybe a hundred lines in two hours. You do it Tuesday through Sunday, twice on Wednesdays and Saturdays, saying the same hundred lines every night. It's like you got stuck in some kinda TV space-show time loop, performing the same actions over and over, dressed in the same clothes, saying the same words again and again. The only difference is that when you were cast, the character was twenty-five and so were you. But now you're forty-nine, and you realize that one day you'll die or get fired; that you'll be gone, but those same actions and words will be repeated night after night, again and again."

"What does any of that have to do with anything we're talking about?" Katrina asked.

"Yeah," I said. "What indeed?"

I stood from the chair, disconnected the phone, and then went out the door.

ALL THE PLAYERS KNEW their parts and lines for the afternoon performance. I could very well be dead before the week was through. So taking a stroll down Broadway seemed like the perfect thing to do.

I walk a lot. But usually my excursions are, in one way or another, connected to a destination. That morning, I had nowhere to go and nothing to run down. So I turned off my phone and ambled.

At Thirty-Second I stopped in a hat shop and bought a

short-brimmed walnut-colored Stetson that I intended to wear as ornament and not disguise.

Half a block south of Twenty-Seventh, I stopped at a pawnshop I'd frequented over the years. Usually the hockshop owner would escort me into the back room, where he kept the firearms.

"Looking for something special, Mr. McGill?" Dido Kazz asked me. He was of indeterminate age, with a receding hairline that formed two horns going back from the brow.

"I was thinking about a pinky ring for my left hand, Mr. Kazz."

This surprised the Greek moneylender.

"But you don't wear jewelry," he challenged.

"Everybody's got to change sometime."

"HELLO, MR. WONG," I greeted the senior host of Madame So's.

"Good to see you, Mr. McGill," he said with feigned warmth if not a smile. "Your party is right this way."

"I've never seen Mama's closed for a private event." I was referring to the small sign affixed to the door downstairs.

"If the clientele is important enough, we sometimes make exceptions." He turned, walking toward a table set for nine.

Twill, Catfish, and Justine were already there. The rest of the dining room was empty.

Twill stood up to clap my shoulder, smiling as always. He would make a great president if our nation were ever *woke* enough to recognize true value.

Catfish and his granddaughter were sitting side by side. Twill and I situated ourselves two seats apart.

"What's that ring?" my son asked.

"Twenty-two-carat gold with a five-carat black-star sapphire. Bought it at Dido's."

"You don't wear rings. And I never seen that hat before either."

"Do you have some kind of plan, Mr. McGill?" Justine asked.

"Of course I do."

"And what is it?"

"This kind of negotiation is not in the telling."

"What is it, then?"

I pretended to consider her question for a full three seconds before saying, "The one thing I need to know before answering you is... What is *your* plan for this meeting?"

Justine's nostrils flared and her eyes widened. She was looking at me, but her focus was far from that room.

"I plan to tell the truth," she said.

"You sittin' there with Catfish on one side and my son

on the other says more than you could ever tell." The smile this statement brought to her lips belonged in one of her grandfather's songs.

She was about to ask something else when Harry Wong brought three more customers to the table. Bernard Shefly, with his arm still in a sling from my son's bullet, was accompanied by Charles Sternman and Hilton Zeal—generally known as the most dangerous criminal on the Eastern Seaboard.

Hilton was six two or more, bearing broad shoulders and an honest-to-God violet suit. His face was unpleasant to look at, but he could have been called handsome in a certain light. He had a truly ugly scar across his right cheek, and his skin color was a white man's version of Catfish's redbone bronze. He pulled out a chair for Sternman, and Shefly pulled one out for him.

Sternman didn't sit at first. He glared at his daughter with something that she must have experienced as vituperation. Seeing his rage and angst made me smile.

Charles stood five eight and had the shape of a hale penguin. His gut was enormous and his hands thick like bricklayers' paws. His eyes were a hazy blue, but still they reminded me of his father's eyes. There was something about the shape of his face that was also reminiscent of the elder.

"I see you met him," Charles said to Justine.

She stared back. There were tremors moving between her neck and her head. The look on her face was spiteful, maybe even with a touch of hatred.

The father lowered into his chair.

"Hello, Leonid," Hilton said. "I've been hearing your name a lot lately."

"Speaking it too," I said.

"You and your son should walk away from this table," Hilton advised. "Walk away and you'll do fine."

"I'm not worried, Zed." I used the letter of his name to show how brave I was. "Reputation can get you into a fracas, but it does not ensure you getting out again."

My knowledge of the alphabet didn't faze him, but I think he was honestly surprised that I did not pick up my marbles and head for the door.

"There's no need for you here," Charles Sternman said, finally looking away from Justine to regard me. "This is a family affair."

"I'm the one who called this meeting," I told the living embodiment of the founding of our nation. "And what it's about is Mr. Catfish Worry and your alliance with these thugs."

"Thugs?" Bernard Shefly said.

"You and your nigger son are nothing," Charles said. I

got the feeling that this was an example of the intermittent release of deep antipathies that had festered in his heart since he was a child.

"Shall we get on with it?" Hilton suggested.

"There are still two empty chairs," I pointed out.

"Who..." Hilton didn't have time to finish the query, because at that moment Harry Wong brought Ernie Eckles and Hush to our table.

"Misters Zeal and Shefly certainly know the man named Hush," I said to Charles. "He's what's known as an iceman, in modern parlance. But they might not recognize our Mississippi friend, Ernie Eckles."

The timing couldn't have been better, and neither could the reactions of the most dangerous criminal in New York and his wounded henchman.

Ernie and Hush filled the chairs between me and my son. Hilton leaned over to whisper something into Sternman's ear.

"What?" the billionaire said.

Hilton shared a few more words.

"So?"

Hilton was about to say more when Sternman shoved him off.

Then Bwana said, "My friend here tells me that you gentlemen are men to be reckoned with, that you are men who wield some kind of power. Well, I want you to know that you have no idea what true power is. I have friends in the FBI and CIA, Mossad and MI6. All I have to do is snap my motherfucking fingers, and people like you disappear." He showed us that he did indeed know how to snap. "But rather than cause unpleasantness, I'll pay you to walk away. This old man is already dead, and the rest of you will join him if you aren't careful. He and you and even these men with me are less than nothing, not worth the sweat off my balls. . . ."

Sternman kept up his escalating rant, spittle popping from his lips, a seemingly uncontrollable sneer mutating every other word. The diatribe caused fear in me; not for myself but for Charles. Catfish was Ernie's mother's friend. The Mississippi Assassin could kill Sternman right then, and there wasn't a man in the room who could stop him—with maybe the exception of Hush. And Hush, I was sure, would not intervene.

I was trying to come up with the words that might quell Sternman, but as it turned out, I didn't have to worry.

"Shut up!" Justine said, rising with the shout.

The astonishment on her father's face told me that she had never stood up to him before.

"We all know your power and your money," she spat.

161

"We know the dangerous men you work with and your whores. No one on this side of the table cares about any of that. Not Mr. McGill or me. My grandfather is your father—that's what's important. I learned that from a letter written on the back of an ancient page torn from the journal of one of our ancestors who came across on the *Mayflower.* The book it came from is in our private library. And that letter was written by your mother, claiming that this man's blood runs in your veins and mine. . . ."

Charles's brow shone with sweat. His fists clenched on the table before him.

"That's why this morning," Justine continued, "before I came here, I sent photocopies of that journal page, back and front, to the *Wall Street Journal,* the *New York* and London *Times,* the *Trib* and *San Francisco Chronicle.* I also sent copies to your friends Thomas Lively, Patrick Foreman, and Marion Lowe. Your close associates who love white people and hate brown."

Charles Sternman got to his feet then. He wasn't as steady as his daughter, but his passion was at least as deep.

"You, you wouldn't," he stammered.

"I did, Father. By the time you get home you will be outed as an African American in every headline, on every news channel. And if anyone challenges it, I'll send out a dozen samples of my blood. My Negro blood."

I was watching at just the moment when Charles Sternman's spirit broke. His healthy skin turned ashen. His superior expression became that of a man pleading with the reality in his mind.

Justine would probably rue her words and actions one day. But that afternoon, she was an exultant Valkyrie.

Charles backed away from the table, knocking his chair to the floor. Then he stumbled toward the exit. His henchmen followed.

Before going out, Shefly turned and pointed at Twill. The gesture seemed to say *I'll be seeing you.*

That was a mistake.

"HE'S ALWAYS BEEN A monster," Justine said over bowls of pork fried rice, black-pepper beef, and sautéed bok choy. Mama So's food is excellent fare. "He abuses everyone, but they put up with it because he's so rich."

Ernie and Hush left a few minutes after Charles and his men.

"Why he hate black peoples so much?" Catfish wanted to know.

"I never understood it," Justine replied. "I always thought that he was so full of spite that he was happy to have anything to hate, from bad weather to the electric bill. He once slapped a boy who kissed me in the summer garden. Hit him so hard that Felix fell to the floor."

"He's my son," Catfish rued. "I should have brung him with me. Ernestine would'a understood."

"I hate him."

They talked like that, back and forth, not really addressing each other. It was as if they were piling dead wood on different sides of a bonfire.

Twill and I ate heartily. At the end, Harry brought out four bowls of bitter melon parfait for desert.

"This is delicious," Justine said of the just slightly sweet pudding.

"What now?" I asked Catfish.

He was looking right through me, calculating the mathematics of loss.

"I guess I done all I could," he said at last. "I got me a new granddaughter an' at least my son knows who he is. Lamont says that he wanna come back to New York an' study at this jazz school you got. Maybe if he study that music, he won't come up with the same answers I did."

"You're going home to Mississippi?" Justine asked.

"That's where my Ernestine is buried."

"Can I come with?"

"What about your fiancé?"

"I'm pretty sure he had his heart set on a white girl."

I TOLD TWILL TO lie low for a few days.

"That's okay, Pops. I got some business to see after in San Diego anyway."

I didn't ask about his business; that's the wisdom of age.

Lamont, Catfish, and Justine left for Biloxi the next day. The men had come by bus, but they returned on a private jet.

For the next few days, I tried to locate Bernard Shefly. I'd taken to sleeping in the office and avoiding Katrina's calls.

On the fourth day, I received a small envelope through the mail. My name and office address were rendered by an ancient typewriter. Inside was a small white card folded in half. The only printing was the word *Condolences* in the lower right-hand corner on the front of the card. Within the fold was a recent article from the *Boston Globe*. A naked corpse with no hands or head had been found near Silver Lake in Newton, Massachusetts. The dead man had been shot in the left shoulder a week or so before his demise.

The card was from either Hush or Ernie; I have my suspicions which one, but it doesn't matter.

The next morning it was announced that Charles Sternman had committed suicide in the night. A week later, there was a photograph in the *New York Times* showing Justine Sternman and an unidentified elderly African American man standing at the graveside. There was speculation about the identity of the man, and his relation to Justine and Charles. One *Post* reporter noted that only the man, whom I knew as Philip "Catfish" Worry, seemed to be near tears.